VERBUM FORTIUS EST QUAM PECCATUM
CUM CULPA DIMIDIATA

STORY SYNOPSIS

When tourists are murdered in a resort town in the northern mountain range of Minnesota, FBI Special Agent Angela Wallace is called in to investigate. But what she finds tests her training and sanity, for what she discovers should not exist.

Winter Kill is the first book in the ongoing werewolf noir series, *The Pack*, by Bram Stoker Award winner Mike Oliveri.

Book two, *Lie with the Dead*, is excerpted in this edition.

WINTER KILL

ALSO BY MIKE OLIVERI

4x4
Collection, with Brian Keene, Geoff Cooper & Michael T. Huyck, Jr.

Deadliest Of The Species
Winner of the Bram Stoker Award for First Novel

To Travel Among Men
From *New Dark Voices*

Warning Signs
From *Brimstone Turnpike*

Werewolves: Call Of The Wild
Comic Book Limited Series

BOOK ONE

The Pack
WINTER KILL

MIKE OLIVERI

AN EVILEYE BOOK
February 2014

Published by
Pulp+Pixel Entertainment Company
301 E. Congress Parkway, #1981, Crystal Lake, IL 60039

Editorial Director: A.N. Ommus

Cover photo illustration, title and book design by Viktor Färro

Red background image: Argus/Shutterstock.com

ISBN: 978-0-9848800-4-1

For more information about this series or other books published by Evileye Books, please visit Evileyebooks.com

Printed in the United States of America.

— 6:23 —

FOR MELISSA

You have kept the faith long past the time
mere mortal women would have told their husbands
to hang it up and chase a real career.

ACKNOWLEDGMENTS

A big thanks to the following people: the rugrats for keeping life interesting; my fellow musketeers, Keene, Coop and Huyck, for existing; John Urbancik for commiserating; Cullen Bunn for the monster margaritas; John Roling, Tim Daly and Shawn Ervin for hollering at me to get work done; Tod Clark and Troy Knutson for being my first nagging fanboys; Minh Nguyen and Kent Gowran for keeping Chicago connections alive; and to my editor, A.N. Ommus and Evileye Books for believing I can pull this off.

You all rock.

WINTER KILL

ONE

KARA KICKED HER TOE INTO A LARGE ROCK, tripped, and sprawled to the ground. Norm hurried back to her side and helped her to her feet.

"Are you okay, Hon?"

"It's getting awfully dark." Kara brushed the grit off her hands. "Don't you think we ought to head back to the campsite?"

"Are you kidding? This is the same time of day the *KenWood* Video was shot. This may be the best time to be looking!"

"I don't think Bigfoot keeps a schedule."

"All the more reason to keep our eyes open. We've only got one more day out here, and I'd hate to go home empty-handed."

Kara shared her husband's enthusiasm for the legendary woodland creature, but she wasn't convinced the grainy *KenWood* Video making the rounds on YouTube and Bigfoot message boards was anything more than a hoax. She wanted to tell him his chances of finding anything were slim to none, even if the grainy video was legit. She wanted to tell him the hikers and hunters packing the lodge after the video went viral on the Web scared away all the native wildlife, including Bigfoot. She wanted to tell him she'd rather spend the rest of their last evening steaming up the tent together than traipsing through the woods.

Instead she let out a restrained huff and muttered, “Fine.”

“What's that?”

“I said—”

“No, no. Listen. What's that noise?”

Kara heard it too: a loud buzz rising in pitch and volume. Norm hefted the camcorder and checked the battery, then kept his thumb hovered over the record button as he scanned the landscape with its night-vision function. The buzz increased to a steady roar.

“That sounds like an engine,” Kara said. “I don't think—whoa!”

Kara shielded her face as the plane soared over their heads, its landing gear nearly kissing the treetops.

“I think it's going down!” Norm said. He turned off the camcorder and shoved it into his coat pocket. “C'mon, they may need help!”

Kara chased him through the brush. “Aren't we near the edge of the lodge's land?”

“So? You don’t want to try to help them?”

“No, I'm just saying the engine was running, maybe there's an airport or something over there.”

“I studied the maps of the area for weeks, Kara. There's no airport.”

“What about private land? A small plane like that wouldn't need much more than a flat stretch of grass.”

“How about we go find out?” Norm snapped. “What're they going to do, get mad at us for making sure they're okay? Now c’mon, they can't be far.”

“Fine.”

TWO

ROD TRIED TO IGNORE THE TREETOPS and the steep, jagged mountain terrain streaking past his window. His pilot was either a genius or a lunatic.

The trip's half done, Roddy. He took one more belt of bourbon from his flask and tucked it into his jacket. Just hang in there.

In front of him, Hank had his boots kicked out under the instrument console and his black Stetson pulled down over his eyes. He snored like a chainsaw. Rod recruited the big man six months after Katrina, and in all the time since, the man did more sleeping than anything else. Like an old coonhound, Hank would wake up long enough to do his job, get something to eat, and find somewhere to stretch out for his next nap.

Hank's partner Jeff, on the other hand, spent all his downtime tending to his pecker. Even now he sat next to Rod with his face buried in a copy of *Leg Show*, reaching down to adjust his package from time to time. With his broad chest and rugged, country-boy features, he could bed the best-looking babes in any given setting. Judging by some of the women Rod had caught him with, however, the guy just wasn't that picky.

Mix the two with a liberal amount of beer and tequila and their hobbies shift to fighting. They grated on Rod at times, but they did what they were told, they were dependable, and they cost him about half what his old New Orleans crew ran him. The latter made their quirks far easier to stomach, even if it meant the occasional foray into the seedier side of redneck nightlife.

The plane lurched and dipped. Rod felt a fingernail bend as he gripped his armrest. He would definitely need another Dramamine before the flight back. More trees streaked past the window, and this time the treetops rose out of sight above him. He closed his eyes. They hit ground, then lifted off slightly as the wheels bounced. Hank muttered something and shifted in his seat. The wheels bounced again, then the whole plane rumbled and shook.

"This thing got four-wheel drive?" Jeff's voice stuttered with the bumps.

"That'd be a good trick with only three wheels, wouldn't it, dumbass?" Marty had a mouth on him, but his rep for flying and his discretion was unmatched. The demand for that particular combination meant his clients either gave him a lot of slack or found other ways to move their product.

Hank chuckled, but Jeff swallowed his pride. For now.

They taxied down the field toward two pickup trucks whose headlights marked the ends of the strip. Marty circled around them and brought the plane to a stop. Rod popped his seatbelt and checked his watch.

"Right on time," he said. "Good job, Marty."

"Of course. Let's get a move on, though. Our flight windows are tight."

"You heard the man, gentlemen. Get your game faces on."

Jeff checked the cylinder of his S&W revolver, then slid it back into the shoulder holster under his flannel jacket. "Ready when you are, boss."

"Alright, then."

The four men climbed out of the plane. To call the strip of flat land an airstrip gave it too much credit, Rod thought. Sure, it was long and flat enough to handle an aircraft, but it was little more than a clearing hacked out of the middle of the Minnesota wilderness. He expected a paved lane of some kind, maybe a maintenance shack or an old barn or hangar; there was none of that. It was a marvel

Marty could find the place at all, but the strip's remoteness also meant few people knew how to find it. The trees surrounding them on all four sides of the strip were a bonus, offering more privacy than Rod could have hoped for.

Marty ducked under the wing with a flashlight and busied himself checking the gears and struts while Hank and Jeff removed a large duffel bag and a hiker's backpack from the cargo space. Rod pulled his denim jacket tighter around his shoulders. He hadn't expected it to be so cold so soon, even this far north, and he regretted not bringing a heavier jacket.

Rod and his men approached the pickups together, none of them flinching at the brightness of the headlights facing them or the shadowed figures approaching to meet them in the clearing between the plane and the trucks. As the men got closer, Rod could see their silhouettes dissolving into clear details: one of the men sported a shaved head and a semi-automatic pistol strapped to his hip; the other, a dirty gray crew cut and peppered goatee. The older man rested the barrel of a shotgun across his shoulder with the business end directed up and behind him, but his finger caressed the trigger guard.

Rod spotted a big guy circling the perimeter with an assault rifle in a ready position, like a soldier on patrol. Dark tattoos adorned his scalp. Another sat behind the wheel of the pickup on the right. He dangled one leg out the side and let the door hang open as he smoked a cigarette. The dome light shined across his bald head.

Rod's business meant dealing with armed thugs, and these guys seemed more interested in putting on a show than using their weapons. Their relaxed demeanor and willingness to approach him demonstrated they didn't intend or expect a double-cross. None of them worried him: if he could see them, he could react to them.

He only sweated the guys he couldn't see.

Baldy and his hip holster stepped out in front of the old guy.

"You Mitch?" Rod asked him.

"You didn't tell us you were a nigger."

Rod looked at his hand. "Still am." The guy just wanted to get a rise out of him, make him lose his cool, and control of the situation. Not gonna happen.

"That supposed to be funny?"

"Is this going to be a problem?"

"We don't deal with niggers."

"I thought you people hated Jews?" Hank said.

Mitch sneered at him. "Mud is mud, cowboy! You'd do well to remember that!"

Hank started toward Mitch, but Rod gave him a "back off" gesture. Hank backed down without breaking eye contact with the big man.

"Listen fellas," Rod told the skinheads, "I don't give a shit about your politics. Fact is, I'm a black man brokering a deal for Mexicans. You need capital, they need guns, and it just so happens my favorite color is the green on the money I'll make. If you really cared where the money was coming from or where the guns were headed, you wouldn't have arranged this deal in the first place. Now, are we going to do this or should I just get back on the plane and tell the Mexicans you pussied out?"

The older man stepped up and leaned in close over Mitch's shoulder. He whispered something, and Mitch nodded.

"Fine. Where's the money?"

"It's in these bags." On cue, Hank and Jeff dropped their packs beside Rod. "The merchandise?"

"Hey there!" All five men turned toward the new voice. "Everything okay?"

The big man on the perimeter raised his rifle to his shoulder and locked his sights on the figure emerging from the thicket of trees.

"Wait!" Rod shouted.

Then everything went to shit.

THREE

"THOSE LIGHTS HAVE TO BE THEM. C'MON!" Norm pushed through the brush a little faster.

They looked more like headlights to Kara. She took a few more steps and looked again, and saw a couple of cars parked in a wide, clear spot. A group of men stood nearby. The headlights shone on the yellow surface of a small airplane.

"Wait, Norm!" She spoke in a harsh whisper. "Something's not right!"

He either didn't hear her or he ignored her and burst through the brush into the clearing.

"Hey there!" Norm gave a big, friendly wave toward the vehicles. "Everything okay?"

Kara heard a shout from the clearing, then a series of loud pops like firecrackers. Something smacked into the trees off to her left.

Oh shit, they're shooting at us! She threw herself onto the ground.

Norm backed into the trees and pulled out the .357 her brother had lent them. "In case you run into bears," he had said. Norm fired in a panic, feeling a rolling heat rush to his face.

The snubby pistol's reports hammered at Kara's ears.

"Run, Kara!" Norm shouted.

Bullets whip-cracked through the air above her.

Norm grunted and fell.

"Norm!" she screamed.

Her husband didn't move.

"There's another one!" someone shouted.

Kara looked up to see a huge man running toward her. She pushed off the ground and ran. A tree branch lashed her left arm, but she kept running. Her heart raced and her ears burned. More bullets zipped around her head a split second ahead of the gunshots. She zigged around a large tree, then zagged across a dip in the ground and sprinted up a short slope through more trees. The gunshots stopped. Maybe he gave up. Maybe he lost her in the brush and the darkness.

Someone punched her in the back. The blow knocked her down, making her crash face-first into another tree.

For an instant, Kara saw nothing but flickering shadows. She tried to draw a breath and a sharp pain dug into her back, just beneath her right shoulder blade. Her arm went numb, and when she tried to push herself up, she flopped over onto her side. Her vision began to blur and grow dark again. She could hear footfalls and the soft, rhythmic clink of metal on metal approaching her from behind.

"Gotcha." A man's voice.

Kara craned her neck around and saw the big man put a rifle to his shoulder.

Another flash and she saw no more.

FOUR

MARTY SLUMPED AGAINST THE LANDING GEAR. He tried to say something but it came out as little more than a gurgle. Rod dropped to one knee at his side and ripped Marty's jacket open. A dark blot the size of a football stained the pilot's white Cowboys jersey. A second later, blood streamed out of Marty's nose and out of the corners of his mouth.

"He's done," Mitch muttered over Rod's shoulder.

The older skinhead came jogging up a moment later. His heaving breaths billowed out like smoke in the frigid air. "Looks like it was just the two. Dane caught up with the woman. The rest of the perimeter is clean."

"Get the crates out of the truck," Mitch told him. "They can load them up themselves."

"Hold up!" Rod said. "We're going to need one of your trucks."

"What the fuck for?"

Rod stood and pointed at Marty. "This was our pilot."

Mitch snorted out a laugh, then turned to his men. "Load up, boys! We're out of here."

"Hey, we had a deal here!" Rod jumped in front of Mitch and pressed a hand to his chest. Probably not the smartest move, but if he had to go back to the cartel empty-handed, these skinheads would be the least of his worries.

"Not any more we don't." Mitch nodded to his men.

The skinheads fanned out. They weren't holding their weapons so casually anymore. The smoker hopped out of the truck and lifted a shotgun to his shoulder. A fifth skinhead ran in from the edge of the clearing, also carrying an assault rifle.

Jeff and Hank drew their pistols and broke away from Rod as he moved to stand over the money bags.

"Fuck this!" The man out of the truck swept his shotgun across the three of them. "I say we waste 'em!"

"Everyone just calm down." Rod held out both hands, palms out. "What's the problem? Is it money? We'll pay you for the fucking truck!"

The old man chuckled. "With what? You gonna find an ATM behind that tree over there?"

"He's got a point," Mitch said. "What's to stop us from leaving all four of you out here to rot while we take our money?"

"Do you think your guys can drop both of mine before they take you down?" Hank and Jeff both turned their pistols on Mitch. Jeff cocked the hammer of his revolver. "If you're dead, how long before they follow the trail back to your guys? Judging by the prison tats on your boy, they won't hesitate to lock him up again."

Mitch's eyes narrowed.

"Don't listen to 'em, boss!"

"Shut up, Dane. What you got in mind?"

"We get out of here together. We do our deal. We go our separate ways. Simple."

"Hey, Duff! C'mere a second."

The old man walked over to his boss. They lowered their heads together and spoke in hushed tones. Rod couldn't make out their words. Behind him, Hank and Jeff kept their pistols pointed at Mitch. Rod willed his crew to stay calm. He worried Mitch's guys couldn't do the same; they jittered like caffeinated teens, sweeping their guns back and forth with no clear aim. Just like sharks in the water, they got their whiff of blood and they hungered for more.

Rod had to admit, were their situations reversed, he'd have already cut the skinheads down and bailed. Now he just had to hope their stupidity trumped their firepower.

"What's it gonna be, Mitch?" Rod asked. "Time's running out."

Mitch scowled at him. He said something more to Duff, and the old man turned around.

"We're out of here, boys!" he told the other skinheads.

"I'm telling you, Mitch, we'll make this worth your while."

"Forget it! This is officially your mess to clean up. You just keep in mind, the cops come knocking at our door, we'll find you."

"What's our play, boss?" Hank whispered.

Mitch and Rod glared at one another, each daring the other to make a move. Their men held their hardware tighter, their muscles tense, ready to snap into action at word from their boss.

"Let 'em go," Rod said, still scowling at Mitch.

Mitch took a few steps back, but his men did not take their guns off Rod.

"You sure?" Jeff asked.

"We don't have much choice."

Mitch climbed into one of the pickups, and his men followed his lead. Rod continued to stare him down as the trucks rolled past.

"Grab the bags," Rod told his crew. "I guess we're walkin'."

FIVE

THE WOLF CROUCHED IN THE BRUSH thirty yards upwind of the buck. He had been stalking it for the better part of an hour. As the buck lapped water from a stream, he saw the opportunity to strike. The hills cast the valley in the plum and golden shadows of the setting sun. The wind grew still.

The wolf bunched its muscles. A leap and a sprint and he'd be on his prey.

Gunshots echoed through the valley. The buck's head snapped up and around. A split second later it was gone, fleeing through the trees to safety.

The wolf already put the buck out of his head. He had a new concern: trespassers. More gunshots rang out. The wolf ran up the valley toward them. It searched and scrambled, stopping from time to time to sniff the air or ground. The guns fell silent, but the wind gave him all the clues he needed. He followed the sound through the trees and over the rolling hills where he caught the faint smell of soap and lavender drifting on the breeze. He followed this new scent deeper into the forest and beyond his own territory, until he caught the scent of blood.

Fresh blood. His heart beat faster.

The scent led him a few hundred yards downhill to a woman lying prone in the dirt, her body still, her eyes fixed in an upward gaze and unfocused. He continued through the downward slope of the hillside until he reached the clearing. There he found a dead man with a revolver still in his grip. The tang of burned gunpowder stung his nostrils. A large shape drew his attention at the far end of the clearing. He looked around for other men who might be lurking, took a few tentative sniffs of the air, then advanced. He saw the prop airplane, but no sign of men around it.

His paws found a dip in the ground, a shallow channel running across his path. The ground around it stank of oil and exhaust fumes. A few feet further on he smelled gunpowder again, and found a spent brass cartridge in the grass. He left it for the moment and continued toward the plane. Yet another man slumped against the landing gear, his hands clutching a dark wound in his gut. The man didn't move or breathe. The wolf already picked up the stink of death that would soon attract the scavengers of the forest.

The wolf circled the plane. The winds told him there were no more men nearby. He returned to the tire tracks. They circled the central part of the clearing, and seemed to come and go through a gap in the trees and a narrow dirt trail. He listened for a moment, but heard nothing, and knew whoever left the scene had a good head start.

He also knew more men would be coming soon. He took one last look around, then disappeared back into the trees.

SIX

ROD CLENCHED HIS TEETH to keep them from chattering. The trail wound from the airstrip downhill through the forest. Tree limbs entwined over their heads and blocked out much of the moonlight. Twice Rod almost fell on his face after tripping on some unseen obstacle on the dark trail. In one spot, their boots sank into mud so thick it threatened to steal Jeff's boots. They heard rustling from time to time, but Rod dismissed the sounds, hoping it was just a fox or a rabbit and not something more dangerous. It would be easy to squash a scorpion in the Texas desert, but he'd be happy to go his whole life without confronting a mountain lion.

It took them almost an hour to reach the road. Rod's fingers and toes had gone from numb to burning as they trekked on toward the south. Jeff and Hank trekked along behind him without complaint, and he started to wonder how much longer he could continue without begging them to carry him.

At last Rod heard a car approaching from behind. He turned and stepped into the lane as the headlights rounded the corner, then waved his arms over his head. The blue minivan stopped beside him and the passenger window went down, slightly.

"You guys okay?"

Rod rested a hand on the passenger door and peered in at the bespectacled man behind the wheel. He was middle-aged, a little heavyset, and he gripped the wheel with calloused knuckles. He had no passengers, but Rod spotted a dirty pink car seat in back.

"We're a little lost." Rod smiled and hoped the guy would take it as humility. "We were hiking in the woods and the batteries in our GPS gave out. We must have taken a wrong turn somewhere."

"Hikers? You must be staying at the Tyler Lodge, then?"

"Yeah, that's right."

"I'm going right by there! Hop in and I'll give you a lift." He reached down and popped the locks.

"Much obliged, mister!" Rod climbed in and relished the warmth of the cabin. He cupped his hands over the heat vents as Hank and Jeff climbed in behind him.

"No wonder you're freezing! That's not near enough jacket for this weather."

Rod forced a chuckle. "I'm from Arizona. I have to admit, I didn't know what kind of cold to expect."

"You're lucky you found the road! Some of these hills go on for miles. People have been known to get lost for days around here!" He turned to face the rear. "How about you boys? Is it warm enough back there? I can turn up the heat if you like."

"We're okay, man," Hank said. "Thanks."

"My name's Ben."

"You live around here, Ben?" Rod pushed past names. The fewer lies he had to tell, the fewer details Ben could give anyone who asked.

"Born and raised. In fact, my father ran the old saw mill up at Miller Station until the shutdown." He went on for a few minutes, providing a Ben-centric history of the area. Rod really didn't give a shit, but he kept him going.

"Sounds like a nice place."

"It ain't much, but it's home. What's life like in Arizona?"

Rod shrugged. "It has its ups and downs. We get a lot of pain-in-the-butt tourists, probably like the lodge."

"Ahh, it's not bad. The Tylers do a good job of keeping them out of trouble. The Tylers themselves, though, they're a bit odd."

"How's that?"

"They're real private folk. Hardly ever leave their grounds, especially after their youngest died a couple years back. Don't get me wrong, everyone's entitled to their privacy. They just seem to take it to an extreme."

"I see."

"Yeah, there's a lot of rumors circulating about that one. I don't want to bore you with gossip, though. Besides, we've just about got you home."

They approached a simple sign announcing the "Tyler Lodge" that listed camping, hiking and hunting. An arrow pointed to a road winding up a hill. Ben turned on to the drive and a few moments later they came upon a large, circular, cabin-style building. Three cars were stationed out front. Through one of the lighted windows of the log building, Rod could see a dining area. A smaller, boxy addition jutted out from one side and a sign over the door indicated the office.

"You guys in a cabin or should I just drop you off here?"

"Right here will be fine," Rod said. "I need to check in with the office anyway."

"Alright, then. You boys enjoy the rest of your stay!"

Ben unlocked the doors. Rod thanked him and agreed that it would be nice if they ran into one another in town. The three of them climbed out and watched the van pull away.

Hank rubbed his ears vigorously with both hands. "I thought he'd never shut the fuck up."

“Sure beats freezing our nuts off,” Rod replied. “Come on, let's see if we can't get some crash space set up.”

A bell jingled over the office door. The interior played up the rustic styling to the hilt, complete with a buck's head mounted over the desk and an animal skin painted with spear-wielding stick figures hunting bison hanging on the wall to the right. Most surfaces in the room demonstrated a carpenter's touch, turning the place into an echo chamber for the thuds from Hank's and Jeff's cowboy boots. If the staff hadn't heard the bell, they surely heard the ruckus.

Rod leaned across the counter. A moment later a bronze-skinned woman came through the back door. She was short and round, and the crow's feet at the corners of her eyes tightened up as she greeted them with a warm smile.

“Evenin', gentlemen,” she said. “I'm Nina. How can I help you?”

Rod matched her smile. “Howdy, ma'am. We were hoping you had a few rooms available.”

“You mean cabins? Do you have reservations?”

Rod made a show of shuffling his feet and looking embarrassed. “Well, that's just the problem. My friends here and I were so intent on getting out here to hike, we each thought the other handled the reservation.”

“Hmm. We've been awfully busy lately, but let me see what I can do for you.” She tapped away at a keyboard hidden below the countertop. "You boys have any problem sharing a cabin?"

Rod punched Hank on the shoulder. "Hank here snores like a foghorn, but I think we can put up with it for a few nights."

Jeff chuckled, and Hank silenced him with an elbow to the ribs.

"How many nights are we talkin'?" Nina asked.

"Four." Rod figured that would be more than enough time to try to recover the deal. If not, he had far bigger problems and a hop over the Canadian border wouldn't be out of the question.

"I might have something." Nina paused, her eyes darting around the glowing screen in front of her. "Here we go. I've got a cabin with a single king-size bed, but we can roll out a cot. Will that work for you?"

"If it keeps us out here among the trees, it's perfect. How much?"

"One forty a night."

Rod wondered if he shouldn't find a cheap motel in the nearest town after all. But with the biting cold and the way his feet hurt, there was no way in hell he was going out again. "Sounds good."

"I'll just need an ID and a credit card, please."

He reached for his wallet. "We'll be paying cash."

"That's fine, but we'll still need a credit card to get you checked in. It's kind of a deposit."

"Ah, no problem." Rod handed over a driver's license and credit card. They identified him as Harold Carter from Reno. The real Harold Carter was a white octogenarian who was in for a surprise if he ever checked his credit report. He always deflected after handing over the card—first step to a successful credit card con. "Do you have any maps?"

"Sure do." Nina handed over a foldout map of the land. It was very detailed, with colored markings, contour lines, and GPS coordinates for important sites. "We can also rent out GPS units for ten dollars a day. I have two left if you're interested."

"Not right now. I'll stop by in the morning if we decide we need it."

"Okay, Mister Carter, I'll just need you to sign here." She handed over his cards, a reservation sheet and pen. She pointed out the lodge's restaurant hours on the sheet, then flipped it over to show them a map of the immediate grounds and pointed out their cabin. "Just follow this road about a half mile, take a right on Sioux Trail and it's about another quarter mile down."

More walking. Swell. "Thanks, Nina! We appreciate it."

"You bet, fellas. Enjoy your stay! If you need anything, just ask."

"Will do. G'night."

Jeff tipped his hat at her on the way out the door. "Ma'am."

When they were out the door and out of earshot, Hank smacked him across the shoulder.

"The hell was that for?"

"Don't even think about it."

Jeff chuckled. "Too late."

"Figures. Hey, boss, where we going from here?"

Rod rubbed his hands together and walked at a brisk trot. "We get warm. Then I try to figure out how we're going to fix this clusterfuck without landing us in a jail cell or a graveyard."

SEVEN

"YEAH, THAT'S HER." Cole stood beside Sheriff Patrick York, watching the paramedics cover Norman and Kara Paulson's bodies. "They were due to check out today."

"Damn." Sheriff York grimaced as he took in their surroundings in the early morning light. "This isn't your land, is it?"

Cole looked around the clearing. He'd visited it once before, several years ago, and even then he'd been curious about the layer of gravel hidden beneath the grass. It had likely been decades since it had last been used as a makeshift airstrip. Now the grasses had reclaimed the ground, but not the trees that were hacked out. Judging by the cut of the grass, someone had come up more recently, perhaps in the last week or so, and cleared everything with a brush mower. The long clippings covered the ground ankle-deep.

"No, but we're probably less than a mile out. We try to be careful not to let folks stray, but you know how that can be."

"Yeah." Sheriff York jotted a few more notes on his pad. "We'll try to keep this quiet. No sense worrying the rest of your patrons."

"Thanks, Pat. I appreciate it."

A lanky deputy with horn-rimmed glasses approached them. "Hey, Sheriff? The ID on the third body checks out."

"And?"

The deputy consulted his notes. "Martin Crowder of Tulsa, Oklahoma. Looks like he was our pilot. He has a few priors for smuggling. The flight plan he filed started in Houston, putting him out near Cheyenne last night."

"Shit." York snapped his notebook closed in frustration.

"What's the matter?" Cole asked.

"This case just went federal."

Cole winced. "Why's that?"

"Three out-of-state victims and a plane in a field two states away from where it belongs. Much as I'd like to keep this in the family, I'm going to have to call this in."

"C'mon, Pat. Maybe the Paulsons here were trying to pull something and the deal went sour. Who'd want to smuggle anything out here?"

"Meth heads, skinheads . . . The list is surprisingly long, my friend. Homeland will probably want a piece of this, too."

"Mm. Well, they need anything, tell 'em I'm happy to help out any way I can."

"I will, thanks. With luck, it'll turn out to be a simple case and over quick. But I've got a feeling we're just scratching the surface here."

Cole headed for his truck.

"Say, Cole?" York called. Cole stopped in his tracks. "Your brothers wouldn't . . .?"

York let the question hang, but Cole got the idea.

"No. Sean's done some stupid shit, but this is well beyond even him."

"I thought so, but I've got to ask. I'm sure the feds will, too."

"If we're wrong, the feds will be the least of his worries."

York chuckled. "I don't doubt it. Say hi to your mom for me, okay?"

"You bet."

Cole climbed into his truck. He drove to the trail and waved to the deputies as he passed their cordon. He waited until he was well out of sight before he punched the dashboard.

EIGHT

"YOU GOT A LOT OF STONES callin' this number, nigger."

Rod bit his tongue. If he could, he'd reach right through the phone and grab the nazi bastard by the throat and squeeze until the fucker's eyes popped. Unfortunately he was the beggar here, so bite his tongue he did, till he could taste the blood. "I've still got your money. You've still got my guns. Let's talk."

Mitch seemed to enjoy Rod's groveling. "Haven't you seen the news? Our little soirée last night is this morning's headline."

"I've been watching it," Rod replied, his tone flat, nonchalant. He had the television on mute at that very moment. "All it tells me is the authorities don't know a thing. If we move fast, we can get this done before they get their heads out of their asses and I'll be gone before you know it."

"Yeah, and leave us behind to carry all the risk. No thanks."

There it is, Rod thought. The angle. The truth. "Alright, how much more is this gonna cost me?"

"Double."

Fucker! "I'll give you another ten."

"Thirty."

Rod felt his ears burning. He exhaled. "Fifteen. Any more and I'll take my chances."

Mitch went silent for a moment. "Deal. When?"

"Give me an hour to make some calls and I'll let you know."

"An hour it is." Mitch hung up on him.

Rod exhaled, dropping his cell phone on the desk.

"Good news?" Hank asked him.

"The deal's back on." Rod turned to the area map he had spread out on the desk. He scanned it with his finger for a moment, then tapped a stretch of road along the far side of the campground. "I've got a job for you. Feel like taking a hike?"

Hank stood and stretched. "Got nothin' better to do. Whatcha got?"

"We need a quiet spot for the meet. Take a walk out here and check it out."

"Can do, boss." Hank picked up his shoulder holster and slung it over his arm.

"I think you should leave that behind," Rod said. "Low profile, remember?"

"Are you kidding? This is Minnesota. At breakfast alone, I spotted three guys packin'. Besides, what if I run into that Bigfoot fella?"

Rod shot Hank a look as he handed over the map. The big Texan winked back at him.

"Asshole," Rod said.

"And then some. See ya in a bit." A chill blew into the room as Hank left the cabin.

In truth, Rod didn't know what to think of the Bigfoot business. The crowd and traffic at breakfast took him by surprise, and just a little eavesdropping told him a fair number of these people were looking for the legendary creature. Only afterward did he notice one of the points on the map was labeled *KenWood* Video Bigfoot Sighting. He worried the crowds would make it tougher to operate unnoticed, but it also made it easier to blend in. Had the campground been empty, the three of them would have drawn suspicion.

He scrolled through the contacts in his phone. Before he could hit the send key, the phone rang. Seeing the number made his stomach churn. People this morning sure were in a reach out and fuck with Rod kind of mood, he thought. He held the phone to his ear.

"Yeah." He knew better than to use Vargas's name on an open line.

"Where is my merchandise?" To Rod, the voice might as well belong to Lucifer himself. There was only one way this conversation could end. But Rod had to plead his case and keep his limbs in one piece. Or at least keep breathing. Maybe he'd offer up Hank or Jeff as sacrificial lambs.

"There's been a complication. Our . . . delivery man has, um . . . taken ill."

Silence.

"Hello?" Rod fished.

"Can you deliver?"

"Absolutely. I just need more time."

"How much time?"

"A couple days. The merchandise is ready. It's just a matter of driving time."

Muffled voices barked on the other end of the line. Rod couldn't make out the words, but one of them sounded terse. At last Vargas got back on the line.

"You have three days. If you do not deliver in that time, we will sever relations. Do you understand me, mayate?"

Dung beetle. The Mexican way to call him a nigger. Once again, Rod bit his tongue.

"I assure you, it won't—" The phone went dead before Rod could finish.

Rod hung up. He sized up his colorful situation:

Nazi scumbags on one side.

Mexican drug dealers on the other.
Momma never said fast money was easy money.

NINE

MITCH SWEATED THE WHOLE RIDE OUT to Minneapolis. He hated to beg, but he didn't see any other choice.

The directions he had been given took him past a refinery and deep into an industrial park. He encountered little traffic as he weaved his way through the maze-like streets, until he found the parking lot of a small tool & die shop near a rail yard. He parked his car near the edge of the lot, then walked two blocks south to the tunnel beneath the railroad overpass.

The entrance sloped down, and just a few yards in, he ran out of daylight. The opposite exit was a bright rectangle of sunlight another hundred feet ahead of him. He walked on the sidewalk between the damp wall and the railing until he reached the halfway point. The sodium vapor lights along the ceiling bathed everything in orange light.

A car entered the tunnel. The weight of the pistol holstered at the small of his back gave him little comfort. The car picked up speed. A moment later he saw a woman behind the wheel and he breathed a sigh of relief. She drove by without making eye contact.

Mitch lit up a cigarette and leaned on the railing. A pickup raced by. The confines of the tunnel reinforced the rumbly noise of its diesel engine, its exhaust fumes hanging in the air. Mitch took another drag off the cigarette. Thank God for menthol.

A dark green Crown Vic entered the tunnel from his right. He watched it approach, and when the driver swung into the oncoming lane, Mitch flicked his cigarette out into the street. The car stopped right in front of him.

"I've got an envelope for you, but I don't see you carrying a bag for me." Detective Nichols wore his badge on a chain around his neck along with gold chains visible under his half-open shirt. He hadn't shaved in days and wore jet black hair so slick, it looked like a helmet. He dangled his sunglasses out the window while glaring at Mitch with his beady black eyes.

"There's been a complication," Mitch said.

"Wait, let me guess . . . that business with the hikers down by Emington?"

Mitch pursed his lips.

Nichols laughed.

"It wasn't our fault. We—"

"Stop right there, because I really don't give a shit. I know the Nation ain't the Boy Scouts, and I know your intentions for this jury list aren't exactly honorable." Nichols held up a brown envelope. "If you really want this, you best cough up my money!"

Mitch stared at the envelope. If the railing hadn't been in the way, he'd be half-tempted to grab it and run. Or maybe just kill the pig right there. Take the envelope and his bling. Maybe the glasses, too, just for spite.

"I can still get the money," Mitch said. "I'll even throw in an extra fifteen K. Call it an apology."

"Yeah? How soon? Your brother's trial starts when, Monday?"

"That's right."

"Cuttin' it kind of close."

"Not seeing much of a choice."

Nichols nodded and looked out toward the tunnel entrance. His fingers drummed the steering wheel.

Mitch's palm itched for the feel of his pistol.

Nichols slapped the dashboard. "An extra fifteen it is," Nichols said at last. "But you need to remember, if I've got the juice to get this list, I've got the juice to make sure your brother has some alone time with some boys from the 'hood. You get me?"

Mitch swallowed and wished it was the pig's blood he was tasting, not his own pride. "Yeah, I got it."

"Good. Have the money Saturday by five. I'll let you know where." Nichols sped away from the curb and back to his own lane.

Mitch walked back to his car. Maybe Dane had the right idea: they should have shot the nigger and his cowboy sidekicks and grabbed the money. If he didn't get that jury list and find a way to bribe or coerce them, he'd be visiting his brother in prison for the rest of his natural life.

Not gonna happen.

One way or another, he'd get that money.

TEN

"WE'RE ABOUT TO RUIN SOMEONE'S DAY."

That's what Shilling said to her as he steered their government-issued Taurus through the winding drive leading towards the Tyler Lodge. Wallace knew he said it meaning it was a good thing. After the Patriot Act, Americans feared and loathed FBI agents more than the phantom terrorists they claimed were crawling all over U.S. soil waiting to strike. Loan shark muscle men were Doctor Phil in comparison to the FBI.

That didn't bother Wallace a bit. She often leveraged it to her advantage.

Shilling parked in front of the office and she pushed the solid oak entry door open without effort. Her partner stepped in behind her, as always. Sheriff York waited in front of the registration desk with a woman by his side.

Special Agent Angela Wallace introduced herself, handed over her business card, then gestured to her partner. “This is Special Agent Brian Shilling.” Wallace was used to taking charge of investigations. It’s how she survived in a bureau full of jackasses and kept local badges from interfering. Shilling had more years in the field, but he’d lost sight of that somewhere and was too content to roll with what others fed him.

“Welcome to the Tyler Lodge. What can I do to help?” The woman beside Sheriff York greeted the agents with a warm smile.

Sheriff York introduced her as Nina Tyler, the owner of the lodge.

Wallace's Jimmy Choo pumps put her a full head taller than Nina; otherwise, they might be the same height. She focused on Mrs. Tyler’s face first. After years in the bureau, Wallace developed the habit of reading a person’s face even before the handshake ended. Those first few minutes were crucial to sizing up what a person connected to an investigation might know—or try to hide. Mrs. Tyler’s face was plump but not fat. She was older than Wallace, with pepper hair and near solid white streaks framing her brown, golden complexion. Her eyes did not avoid eye contact with Wallace. She could be sincere or it could be a well-rehearsed line. York stood off to one side and turned the brim of his Smokey hat through his fingers. Wallace noticed the subtle gesture and couldn’t help but wonder if he was sweet on Mrs. Tyler or if he just felt bad for bringing the feds into her lodge.

"We'd like to see the Paulsons' campsite as soon as possible. It would also be helpful if you could put us up for the night; we'd like to stay close to the crime scene while we conduct our investigation."

"Of course." Nina stepped around the front desk and went straight to her computer. "We have a cabin that opened up this morning. It should be cleaned up by now. It's got a king-sized bed and a couch, if that's okay?"

"That'll be fine. Agent Shilling's the chivalric sort and will be happy to sleep on the couch."

Shilling let out a short cough behind her. Wallace cracked a smile, but erased it before Nina looked back up at her.

"Who checked out of that cabin this morning?"

Nina looked over at York. He gave her a nod. "No problem. Let me grab a couple keys for you and I'll get one of my sons to take you out to the Paulsons' site." Nina picked up a Motorola two-way radio as she turned to the key rack behind her. "Ronnie, you out there?"

There was a click of static, then the response: "Yeah, Ma. What's up?"

"Where are you?"

"Out in the shed."

"Great. Can you come up to the lodge?"

"Be right there."

"He's on the way over. Here're the keys . . ." Nina set the keys on the countertop, then tapped at the keyboard for a moment. A laser printer hummed to life, and when it quit again she set a sheet of paper beside the keys. "And here's the information about the folks who left this morning."

Wallace tossed one of the keys to Shilling, then looked over the printout. It listed the cabin to Shawn Ervin, Des Moines, Iowa. "How about late arrivals? Anyone come in last night?"

"I was just thinking about that." The printer hummed again. "Here we go. This guy came in late last night."

Wallace looked at the new sheet. "The Visa card clear?"

"The hold went through. We haven't charged anything to it yet."

Wallace nodded and folded the two pages together. The door chimed as she tucked them into her jacket, and she turned to see a tall, dark-skinned man come through the door. Despite the stern expression usually reserved for older men, Wallace could see that he was young, in his twenties. She also noticed the resemblance between him and his mother, especially around their piercing brown eyes. Straight black hair framed his face and hung to his shoulders.

Sheriff York touched Ronnie on the shoulder while pointing to her and Shilling. "Ronnie, these folks are federal agents."

"Special Agent Angela Wallace." She put out her hand and he shook it with a powerful squeeze that made her knuckles ache. He shook Shilling's hand as well, noticing the tension in their wrists.

"How you doing, Ronnie?" York asked.

"Not bad, Pat. You?"

"No complaints. These fine folks would like to see the Paulson campsite. Can you take us out there?"

"Didn't your boys already take care of things this morning, Sheriff?"

"We'd like to take a look ourselves," Wallace didn't give Sheriff York a chance to respond. She hated being ignored.

As the group made their way out, Wallace ignored Mrs. Tyler. Let the matriarch stew a little, she thought. The routine was playing out as always. Now Wallace just needed to watch and wait. Eventually, they all cave under the pressure.

Ronnie was next.

ELEVEN

WALLACE CAUGHT HER PARTNER'S EYE as they walked out of the lodge. She made a driving gesture and pointed to him. He nodded and headed for the driver's side door of the Taurus. As she slid into the back seat, Wallace watched Sheriff York and Ronnie catch up to them. They didn't seem in a hurry. Turned to one another slightly, they talked in low enough voices for Wallace to miss what they were saying.

Wallace watched them. Ronnie didn't seem to have a problem with the local police presence, but something bothered him about her and Shilling being there. Her hand still ached a little from his handshake, which seemed to her a challenge or a show of dominance. Despite his downplay, Ronnie was clearly agitated. She was looking forward to the interrogation.

Ronnie walked to her side of the car and she pointed at the front passenger seat. He went around the back and climbed in next to Shilling where she could keep a close eye on him.

She watched Sheriff York get into his patrol car and wait for them to pull out.

Shilling barely made it past the lodge's welcome sign before Wallace dug in on the questions. "So your family runs the place then, Mr. Tyler?"

"That's right." Cold. No hint of pride, Wallace thought.

"This is very pretty land out here. There must be a lot of upkeep for just your family, no?"

Ronnie shrugged. "It's a little busier than normal right now, but we hire out when we have to. Especially during the hunting seasons."

"Is it just you and your folks?"

"Myself, my brothers and my mother. My father's dead."

"Sorry to hear that."

Ronnie shifted in his seat and sat a little straighter. "It was a long time ago."

She took a quick glance at her notes from the scene of the shooting. "So it's just you, Cole—that's your older brother, right? And . . .?"

"Sean."

Wallace wrote their names near Cole's, then added Nina—Mother. "No girls, eh?"

"My sister goes to college in Illinois."

"Ah. What's her name?"

"Diana."

"And you had another younger brother as well. He died in Nevada a couple of years back, correct?"

"That's right." Ronnie looked outside at the passing hillside and foliage. "Is there a reason you're asking all these questions?"

"Just making conversation."

Ronnie turned and looked over his shoulder at her. "Then why are you writing it all down in that notebook?"

"Never know what will come in handy."

"What tribe are you from Ronnie?" Shilling asked. Shilling was on cue: deflecting to keep the information flowing. Their version of good cop, bad cop.

Ronnie settled back into his seat. "My father was Lakota. Turn right between those trees."

"No shit? I'd have guessed you were from one of the local tribes. Ojibwe, maybe. You associate with them at all?"

"Not really. Mom's Navajo, so we aren't exactly local blood."

If she kept this up, she knew it wouldn't be long before Ronnie made a mistake. Then they saw the flashing lights just up the trail.

"That's the campsite up ahead."

She made note of the relief in his voice.

TWELVE

A CRUISER PAINTED IN THE BROWN AND GOLD county colors was parked just off the path to Wallace's right. Yellow police tape created a cordon around a boxy blue tent, a fire pit, a picnic table and a red Prius. It didn't look any different from any other campsite she'd ever seen, but it didn't hurt to take a look. A deputy climbed out of the cruiser as they pulled up next to it.

Wallace rolled down her window. "Have you removed anything?"

"No, ma'am."

York was already making his way toward them as Wallace climbed out of the car, pointing to a cloth bundle and some food spread out on the ground. "We cut that down and looked through it, but otherwise we haven't touched a thing."

"Cut it down?" Shilling asked, already standing beside Wallace and Ronnie.

"We ask campers to hang their food items from a tree," Ronnie explained. "It's a safety precaution against bears."

"I see." Wallace poked through the bundle with her toe as she pulled on some rubber gloves Shilling handed her from his jacket pocket. He put on a pair as well, crouched and dragged a basket out from beneath the picnic table.

The Paulsons kept a tidy site. Wallace spotted the remains of aluminum cans amidst the campfire ashes, and a trash bin near the table had already been emptied. The interior of the tent had also been well kept, with a bag of toiletries, a suitcase and a lantern near the door. Wallace searched the bag and found a short stack of books, each about mythical monsters or Bigfoot. She flipped through one and saw several fuzzy photographs, crude drawings, and pictures of footprints. One picture with the caption Bigfoot scat caught her eye and chuckled.

She carried the books outside, handing them to Shilling. "Check this out."

"Bigfoot? We got some obsessives here?" Shilling said with a smirk.

"That would be why we've been so busy lately," Ronnie said.

"You're kidding," Shilling knew he wasn't, but he was sticking to the good cop script.

“Nope. Some campers thought they spotted him about a month back. They posted some video to the Internet. People have been showing up in droves ever since.”

“Have you seen this video?” Wallace asked. Sheriff York came closer.

Ronnie shrugged. “Yeah, but what they recorded could be anything, if you ask me. It's just a cell phone video. It's real grainy.”

“But you're not discouraging anyone from showing up,” Wallace didn’t look at Ronnie when she laid the bait, just kept on rummaging through the site remains. But she was paying attention. Her ears were perked. His answer would reveal a lot.

“Business is business. To be honest, it's both a blessing and a curse. We're bringing in some cash, but we've had to work our butts off to cover the traffic.”

Wallace was disappointed. She’d hoped Ronnie would tip off a tell of some kind. But he didn’t. His answer was straightforward—earnest even. If he was hiding any information, she would’ve caught a hesitation, a quick glance away, or even Sheriff York coming to the rescue. But she got nothing.

Wallace set the books on the table while they finished searching the site. She dumped the laundry bag, searched the sleeping bags, pillows, even the contents of the bottles in the toiletries. After a few minutes, she stood straight and stopped her search. She sniffed a dead end.

"Sheriff, have you contacted the next of kin?"

"Not yet."

"Go ahead." Wallace saw no point in wasting any more time on the site or the dead couple. Let them rest in peace. She began to roll off the plastic gloves. "If you would, please have your men pack up the site and secure the contents. Let's hold off on releasing the Paulsons' names to the media for now, but release the details on the plane and the pilot. Maybe that will turn something loose."

Shilling slammed the car door and removed his gloves. "Car's clean."

"Alright. Let's do a quick perimeter search, out to about a hundred feet. Let's make sure we haven't missed anything in the trees. Sheriff, if you and Ronnie would start that way, my partner and I will start back here."

Sheriff York nodded to Wallace and started his search with Ronnie toward the sloping thicket of trees.

Wallace didn't like that the site was clean. When they first arrived, she hoped for a quick case. The more twisting trails and dead ends, the more likely they would never solve it. So far, all leads were cold. The Tylers seem to be clean. And all she could tell from the sheriff is that he might or might not have a thing for Mrs. Tyler. Maybe Shilling had some ideas.

THIRTEEN

WALLACE AND SHILLING WALKED into the thicket of trees together, scanning a few feet at a time in front of their feet, waiting to be out of earshot. After a while, Wallace asked her partner, “What's your take?” This is why she liked having him as a partner. No matter what the situation, he always managed to stay level-headed. Objective.

“I'm thinking the Paulsons were in the wrong place at the wrong time. The plane's empty. So, whether Crowder was dropping off or picking up, someone's still running around with merchandise and/or payment.”

“And the Tylers?”

“The guy's definitely not happy we're here. You think they may have been the contact point?”

"It's possible. Even if the land's not theirs, it's convenient. No reason they couldn't have cleared out that airstrip without any of their patrons noticing. On the other hand, it would be awfully ballsy to pull off some kind of deal with the extra tourists around."

"How do you want to play it?"

Wallace pulled the two printouts from her jacket. "Let's call in these names, then I'll have the good sheriff pull whatever he can about the Tylers."

"He seems friendly with them. He may not like you snooping."

"Who gives a shit? He gives us a hard time, we'll threaten him with obstruction."

Shilling laughed. "You're always good at making friends."

FOURTEEN

THE LAST THING RONNIE WANTED TO DO was talk. He'd had enough of it with that agent Wallace. He was sure the family was in the clear. He sensed it back at the Paulson camp, as they fanned out into the woods: by the unsure way she walked; her slightly sloping shoulders; her constant looking over at her partner, Shilling, as he spoke; the take-charge attitude gone. Still, he wasn't convinced that meant the FBI was going away.

"We need to talk."

Cole didn't bother to look up. He just kept flipping the burgers on the sizzling grill. "Go ahead."

It was always the same with Cole: you had to blast through concrete to get his attention. Ronnie spoke in hushed tones, leaning in close. "Damn it, I mean somewhere private."

"Alright, then." Cole asked one of the other cooks to cover the grill, then stepped outside with his brother. "What's the problem?"

"These feds snooping around. They even asked about Will and Nevada. What are we going to do if they get the whole story?"

"It's not a question of if, Ronnie. They probably know already. We just need to stick to the same story we put together for Pat and everyone else. As long as we're consistent, it's not going to matter what happens with the FBI now."

"Yeah? And what about Hess? What keeps him from running his mouth the moment the feds start sniffing around?"

"He doesn't want to go to jail any more than I do."

"It's not about jail time and you know it!" Ronnie shouted. He looked around, then leaned in closer to his brother and spoke in a harsh whisper. "That son of a bitch has a hell of a story to tell. You should have killed him when you had the chance."

"If I'd killed him, it would have been a lot harder to explain away the rest of the bodies."

"Goddamn it, he killed our fucking brother!"

Cole grabbed Ronnie's jacket and slammed him against the wall. The impact rattled the door and Ronnie let out a whoosh of breath.

"You think I don't know that? You didn't have to find Will buried in a fucking gravel pit, I did! You think I wanted to walk away from that?" Ronnie tried to pull Cole's wrists away, but his grip was too strong. A familiar heat began to fill his head. Cole pressed his brother harder against the wall. "This is the last time I'm going to have this conversation with you. I used my head, not my gut, and I did what's best for this family! Now if you just shut your mouth and trust me, we'll get through this."

The door slammed beside them. Nina Tyler popped her head out. "Boys!" she snapped. "What's going on out here?"

Cole released Ronnie's jacket. "Nothing we can't handle."

Ronnie glared at him. The conversation wasn't over.

"Whatever the problem, you need to end it. Right now."

Ronnie straightened his jacket with a forceful tug.

Nina motioned to Cole. "Agent Wallace wants to speak to you."

"No problem." He glared at Ronnie. "Keep your cool and we'll be fine."

Ronnie shoved him away and took a few steps back. There was no more panic. Now he was just angry at Cole for not taking charge. For not seeing it his way. "Just remember you're not the old man."

Cole watched his brother leave, then untied his apron. "Where's the fed?"

"I set them up in the office," Nina said. "What was that all about?"

"Will."

FIFTEEN

THEY WAITED FOR HIM IN HIS OWN OFFICE. Wallace thought being in a comfort zone might make him slip. But she wanted to see him squirm a little, so she sat behind his desk—see what he does with that one, she thought. She knew Shilling wouldn't object; he was used to her pulling her power plays. That's how they usually caught their man.

But when Cole came into the room, her breath caught in her throat. He stood at least as tall as his brother, Ronnie, but carried a lot more muscle, his broad shoulders almost spanning the width of the doorframe. His square jaw and the general cut of his body reminded her of a large, chiseled sculpture, hard and immovable. The earthy type was an understatement. His bronze flesh matched his mother's. He wore his black hair in a ponytail that swayed forward as he reached out to shake her hand.

“I'm Cole Tyler. You folks wanted to talk to me?”

Wallace gawked.

Cole looked at her then at Shilling with raised eyebrows. Finally, Shilling stepped around her and offered his hand to Cole.

“Mr. Tyler, I'm Special Agent Brian Shilling. Nice to meet you. This is my partner.”

“I’m Angie—” She caught herself and shook it off. “Special Agent Angela Wallace!” Cole’s huge hand engulfed hers. He gave it a firm but gentle squeeze. When he let go, she gestured to her chair in front of the desk. “Please, have a seat.”

Shilling moved around behind Cole and closed the door. He caught Wallace's eye and raised an eyebrow at her.

Cole sat with his right foot propped across his knee. His eyes roamed the office.

“Something wrong, Mr. Tyler?” Shilling asked as he returned to the chair beside the desk.

“I'm used to sitting on the other side of my own desk, that's all.”

“Ah, sorry about that,” Wallace said. “We felt it would be more convenient than dragging everyone down to the police station in town.”

Cole shrugged. “Whatever works for you.”

Shilling held up a digital voice recorder. "You mind if we record this?"

"Nope."

Shilling thumbed a button and the red LED lit up. Wallace recited the date, time and location, and listed all of their names. She then asked Cole to confirm his consent for the recorder, and he did. She dug into her list of questions.

"Mr. Tyler, can you tell me where you were between the hours of seven and ten p.m. last night?" Wallace asked.

"I was working in the kitchen 'til a little after nine, then I made a few rounds of the campground with Shawn."

"Can anyone confirm that?"

"Shawn, for starters, the other cooks, and maybe a few of our visitors."

Wallace nodded and jotted a few notes in her notebook. "How about your brothers?"

"Ronnie spent most of that time in the shed."

"Meaning?"

"We've been having trouble with our pickup. We use it for emptying the trash barrels at all the campsites, and Ronnie had to do some emergency repairs."

"Is your brother a mechanic?" Shilling asked.

"He can handle a wrench."

"But he's not been trained, correct?" Wallace asked.

"No, ma'am. We got our start working on our bikes, and Ronnie kept going bigger. Now he fixes the truck, the water pumps, whatever."

"I understand your sister . . ." Wallace checked her notes. "Diana is the first of your siblings to graduate from high school, not to mention go to college. Why is that?"

"Dad always taught us to be self-sufficient. My brothers and I never had much use for school, so Mom home-schooled us."

"Such a large family? That's impressive."

"Mom used to be a teacher. She made it work."

"I see." Wallace paused. She was done with the small talk. Time to unfurl the big red flag she found in Sheriff York's files. "Tell me about Nevada."

"Hmm. It's still kinda hot this time of year. Lots of sand blowing around . . . a bit dry for my taste." Wallace scowled, and Cole chuckled. "I'm kidding. I assume Pat—sorry, Sheriff York—gave you the scoop?"

"He did, but I'd just as soon hear it straight from the source."

"Alright. Will and his fiancée, Kate Henrikkson, went to Vegas to get married. When we didn't hear from them for a while, I went looking for them. Unfortunately, I found them in Sunset, Nevada, where a man named Marcus Rice had murdered them."

"I understand you found the bodies?"

"The Sunset police chief, Sheriff Hess, and I went out to the mine together. I happened to find the site before he did. That's when Rice jumped us. There was a struggle and Sheriff Hess shot him."

"Why would Rice want to kill your brother?"

"Apparently, he was psychotic. He killed a deputy that same night. Hess later proved Rice killed his own brother, too."

Wallace leaned back in her chair. It sounded good, but it didn't ring true. "But Mr. Tyler, Sunset is only a couple hours from Vegas. Why would your brother and your future sister-in-law stop in a speck of a town like Sunset with the sights and sounds of the Sunset Strip just a little farther away?"

"Couldn't tell you," Cole said. "I never had a chance to ask him. I assume they were tired and decided to stop."

Wallace and Shilling shared a look.

"What do you think, partner?" she asked.

Shilling pursed his lips for a moment. "Mmm, I don't know, Prince puts on a pretty goddamn good show. I'd much rather catch the Purple One on stage than watch tumbleweeds blow through town."

"Will wasn't much of a Prince fan," Cole said with a chuckle, "but I see your point. As I said, I didn't get a chance to ask him."

"Fair enough," Wallace said. "Let's talk about Sean."

"Can't say he much likes Prince, either. That's well before his time."

"Cute, Mr. Tyler. I meant his prior convictions."

"What, the weed thing?"

"That's right."

Cole rolled his eyes. "He got nailed toking up with a few of his buddies in town. He was a dumbass teenager."

"The police report said he was the supplier."

"Yeah, he found marijuana growing out on a hillside somewhere and cut some of it down."

"Is it still growing out there?"

"I see where this is going," Cole said. "You think the plane was making a pickup, is that it?"

Shilling smirked.

"It's not a tough conclusion to reach," Wallace said.

Cole nodded. "I suppose not, but let me save you some time—you're pissing up a rope. The DNR helped us burn out that crop, and we haven't seen anything since."

"Pity. I would think drug profits could go a long way toward providing self sufficiency."

"You might think. Jail time, however, does not. We about done here?"

"You got a plane to catch?" Shilling asked.

"Hilarious. Actually, I've got a campground full of hungry customers and I left the griddle undermanned."

"I think we're done for now," Wallace said.

"Great." Cole stood. "I realize you're just doing your jobs

and all, but you let me know when you're ready to be productive, okay?"

Wallace put on an exaggerated, forced smile. "We'll do that, Mr. Tyler."

"Have a good night."

Shilling followed Cole to the door and shut it behind him. "I don't think our friend there is telling us the whole story."

Wallace reached over and turned off the recorder.

"I don't doubt that. I'm not seeing any reason to connect them to the plane yet, but something's up. Do we know who owns the land the airstrip was on?"

"York was supposed to scare up the county recorder to look it up. I haven't heard back yet."

"Alright. Let's take a ride into town and turn over some rocks, maybe get something to eat."

"What, suddenly Tyler's not good enough to cook for you?"

Wallace laughed. "I'd rather not have a wad of phlegm in my burger."

SIXTEEN

JEFF COULDN'T REMEMBER when the habit started, but whenever he and Hank walked into a place, Jeff sized up the joint based on its decor. Not that he swung that way, but the layout of a place told him two things straight away: the fastest way out and where the liquor flowed.

The lodge interior had a little of everything, but Jeff felt like it just couldn't find an identity for itself. The huge, circular area had probably been intended for a communal feel at some point, but over time it seemed the owners subdivided it to cater to different tastes. The front had a lobby vibe going for it, with couches and stools placed along a stone-tiled floor leading to the center, where there was more seating and a fireplace. A large stone chimney rose up to the center of the roof. The fire opened onto two sides. A four-foot wall topped with a glass partition divided the bar and restaurant side from the rest of the room, and a small rec area with a pool table and arcade took over the back section. Another short wall partitioned the remaining open space and a small platform for conferences and other events. What a clusterfuck, he thought. Just like the deal with the skinheads.

Hank slunk down next to him and ordered a shot of whiskey and a beer for Jeff before his ass kissed the chair. Jeff followed and continued to scope out the place. Bad habit, even when he wasn't on the clock. But he couldn't help. Most of the lodge's tenants had already cleared out for the night, leaving a handful of people to finish their dinners in the restaurant; a couple more guys playing darts in the rec area talking about the *KenWood* tape; a gray-haired man with a white bush 'stache had fallen asleep on a couch near the fireplace; two younger, blueblood types sat opposite him smoking cigars, just staring at the old man drool down the side of his mouth like he was their main attraction for the evening. What a lively bunch.

Jeff swirled the last of his beer around his glass. All in all, the place was dead. Deader than dead. Would it kill them to have installed a jukebox and stocked it with some Jennings or Cash? Hell, he'd be happy with the pop crap they passed off as country these days if it would get some of the women up and dancing. Most of them seemed attached to a dweeb or a dipshit, but every so often Jeff's eyes wandered over to two women sitting near the bar.

The leggy blonde had been stealing glances at him for the past fifteen minutes. He put her around twenty-five, and despite her acne problem, the swell of her sweatshirt gave the promise of plenty hidden beneath. Her brunette friend carried a little extra weight, which she tried to hide under a loose, draping jacket. She had a round, pretty face, though, and piercing green eyes. Too bad he couldn't swap their heads, giving him a knockout and her cast-off friend. Jeff didn't have much use for unique attributes in a woman, as long as he could get some action before he died of boredom.

Blondie caught him staring and gave him a smile and a nod. Brunette leaned across the table, whispering something urgent into her friend's ear.

He supposed Blondie would have to do.

" 'Scuse me for a bit, Hank." He downed his glass and stood up.

Hank followed his gaze across the room to the girls and back. "Aw, c'mon, Jeff. This ain't the time."

"Like hell. Rod told us to relax for the night, and that's exactly what I'm gonna do."

"Anything I can do to dissuade you?"

"Nope."

"Then I reckon you'll need a wingman."

"Good man."

Jeff and Hank carried their glasses over to the girls. Blondie smiled and sat back in her chair. She crossed her arms, but she also crossed her right leg over her left knee and bounced it vigorously, drawing in Jeff's gaze straight up to her crotch. The brunette sat up straight and looked away from them. A blush crept into her cheeks. She looked like she wanted to jump up and run away.

"Evening, ladies!"

"Hi there," Blondie said.

"I'm Jeff, and this is my friend Hank." He pulled a chair over from the next table and turned it to face the women.

"I'm Emily," said Blondie, "and this is Jennifer," but Jeff didn't care. He was thinking up names for the mounds under her sweatshirt.

Jennifer kept her face turned toward the last few bites of chocolate cake in front of her, offering only a half-assed wave in greeting.

"What are you ladies doing here all by your lonesome?"

"The guys went—"

"Our boyfriends," Jennifer interjected.

"Your boyfriend and his buddy Devan," Emily retorted, "wandered off with some guys from another campsite."

"Well that doesn't make any sense, does it Hank?"

"Nope. None at all."

"What could possibly be more interesting than spending a night with a couple of sweet young things like yourselves?"

"Bigfoot," Emily said.

"You're shittin' me."

"Nope. We were supposed to be spending three nights in the 'shadow of the monster!' " She said the latter in a mock creepy voice, as if from a bad movie trailer. "Instead, the boys ran into some supposed Bigfoot hunters, and next thing we know they're all sitting around talking about making some kind of movie."

"Web series," Jennifer said.

"Yeah, that's so much better. The point is they abandoned us."

"Can we buy you a few drinks to ease your pain?" Jeff waved over the waitress.

"I thought you'd never ask."

"What's your pleasure?"

"Surprise me."

The waitress came over to the table. "What can I get you?" Jeff flashed her smile. He liked her dimples, but she wasn't having any of it.

"Bring us two boilermakers, and for the ladies, let's go with . . . two hot chocolates with a double shot of Schnapps."

Emily cocked her head to one side as she considered the order.

"Oh, wait, I don't want any," Jennifer told the waitress.

"Why not?" Hank asked her.

"You don't need to buy our drinks."

"It's not about need. We're just being friendly."

"It's very kind of you, but our boyfriends—"

"You like hot cocoa, don't you?"

"Well, yeah . . ."

"Then relax and enjoy." Hank held up two fingers to the waitress. "Two, please."

Jennifer looked up at the waitress.

"It's up to you," the waitress said. Her tone seemed to say I wouldn't. Jeff thought she had that uppity look about her, like she was tired of even flirting for tips. She looked like she'd have been a good time back in the day, but years of shucking dinner plates and swapping bottles had caught up with her.

"I'll try one," Jennifer said at last.

"Suit yourself. I'll see what we can scare up."

Throughout the exchange, Jeff looked Emily in the eye, daring her to read his intentions. He could see the curiosity burning in her head. At last she asked the question.

"Why hot chocolate?"

"It's simple." Jeff ticked his rationale off on his fingers. "Something hot for a cold night, every lady finds comfort in chocolate, and the Schnapps is for some flavor and fun."

"I'm impressed."

Jennifer rolled her eyes. "C'mon, Em. Don't you think he's laying it on a little thick? He's just trying to get in your pants."

Emily rubbed her foot along the side of Jeff's leg.

"Then he's on the right track."

SEVENTEEN

ROD HAD NO OTHER WORD FOR WHAT HE SAW.

Boneheads.

He watched Mitch and his man Dane climb out of the pickup and approached Rod as he leaned on the hood of the rental car. Mitch covered his bald head with a knit cap. He wore jeans and a nondescript green jacket. Dane, on the other hand, loomed over his boss like a giant. The prison tattoos on his temples stood in stark contrast against his pale flesh. The collar of his sweatshirt had been torn off to reveal the swastika tattoo near his throat and a hint of the Nazi eagle spreading its wings across his chest. A huge handgun dangled from a holster at his right hip.

"The very picture of discretion," Rod groused under his breath.

"What's that?" Mitch asked.

"I thought we agreed to meet alone?"

"You did. We didn't. This the place you had in mind, then?"

"It is. What do you think?"

"Dane, walk the perimeter?" The big man grunted something and trotted into the woods. Mitch lifted his jacket to display a .45 slotted into his waistband. "Is he going to run into any surprises out there?"

Rod sighed. "Like what?"

"You best not be fuckin' with us, boy."

"Look, man, what good would it do me to jump you tonight? You're not going to have the gear on you, and you're the one who wanted to see the place beforehand. I'd just as soon be back at my cabin having some warm chow about now."

"You calling me an idiot? Because the way I see it, you could be buying some time for your backup to arrive."

"Of course not! I told you on the phone: I need to wait on the money and the transportation. Texas isn't exactly close! Why do you think we brought the plane to begin with?"

"U-Haul not good enough for you?"

"Wow, brilliant!" Rod smacked the heel of his palm to his forehead. "Let's use a completely traceable service that requires identification and credit cards! Think, man! Do you really want a paper trail connecting us if something goes wrong?"

Mitch's eyes narrowed. For a moment Rod thought the man would draw his gun and shoot him dead on the spot. At last, Mitch turned around and looked up at the trees and the hillsides around them.

The hollow lived up to Hank's description and then some. Situated on the far western edge of the lodge grounds, it ran straight for a hundred yards or so, then curved around to the north toward the highway, another quarter mile away. A hiking trail came down from the hill, crossing the highway. The guardrail protecting the trail from the highway left a gap in the shoulder large enough for a vehicle to squeeze through. With a little careful driving, it was easy to get off the trail and down an easy slope into the hollow. Behind Rod, the hollow wound through the trees and rejoined the lodge's main hiking trails. On his way to the meeting, the rental car almost got stuck in a patch of mud as Rod entered the valley, but otherwise the car handled the valley floor just fine. The tall hills flanking the hollow and the trees growing from their slopes afforded them plenty of privacy, more so than even the airstrip had.

“What do you think?”

“It could be plenty messy if one of us decides to screw the other,” Mitch said.

“There's enough heat here. Upping the body count won’t help.”

Dane trudged back down the hill and across the riverbed. "Seems he came alone. I don't see any campers around, either."

"And the lodge wants everyone back at their campsites by ten o'clock," Rod said. "We should have this spot to ourselves after that."

"Fair enough. We'll be back tomorrow night. Dane, give the man a kiss, would you?"

Dane grinned and grabbed Rod by the front of his jacket.

"Wait! What're you—"

Dane pulled Rod forward and at the same time rammed his forehead into Rod's nose. A painful crunch rocked his face, then all Rod could see was black and wild shooting lights. Blood gushed over his lip. Dane, still grinning, dropped him onto the hood of the rental car.

"That's for being an asshole," Mitch said. "C'mon, let's go."

Rod pinched his nose and let his head hang forward. It stung, but he didn't think his nose was broken. At least he hoped; last thing he needed was to walk into an emergency room. He watched the skinheads get in their pickup, turn it around and drive out of the hollow, leaving the dust their tires rustled up hanging in the air and clinging to the drying blood on Rod's face.

"Goddamn nazis," Rod muttered.

He waited a moment, then coughed up blood. He still felt a trickle in his nose, but it seemed to stop bleeding.

Carefully, he removed the brand new jacket Jeff had picked up for him in town and used the side of his shirt to clean up his face and hands. He double-checked his cleanup job in the side mirror of the rental before putting his jacket back on, then got in the car. Still sniffling, he looked back into the mirror.

"Remind me to get out of the gun-running business," he told his reflection. Then he nodded once and started the car.

With a little luck, the kitchen would still be open back at the lodge and he'd be able to get something to eat.

EIGHTEEN

WALLACE PUSHED HER DINNER PLATE AWAY and rubbed her eyes. She didn't think it was possible to screw up something as simple as a corned beef sandwich, but this cook had figured out a way. She ate it just to fill her stomach. The fries on her plate were too greasy to eat. At least the coffee didn't taste like tar.

Sheriff York told her and Shilling the diner would be the only place still open, so their options were limited unless they wanted to head back up to the lodge for dinner. The booths and chairs looked like they hadn't been updated since the Carter administration, and a thick layer of dust coated the top edges of the old-fashioned Coke bottle cap signage on the walls. The VFW next door had just wrapped bingo night, and a swarm of old folks began to fill the tables. Most of the seniors reeked of cigarette smoke.

They bitched and moaned as the waitress tried to keep up with their orders.

The door chimed and a burly, bearded man stumbled through. Wallace watched him lean against the back of the nearest booth and look around the room. Though he wore a cap that shadowed his eyes, she could see trails of dried tears down his dusty cheeks. The filth of a hard day's work stained his hands and his quilted flannel shirt. When he spotted Wallace and Shilling he squinted for a moment, then weaved through the crowd toward them. Wallace gripped her coffee mug a bit firmer. She sensed heads turning their way.

“Heads up, Brian.”

Shilling set down his burger and pushed away from the table a few inches.

Wallace wasn’t sure of the old man’s intent, but his stride toward them was too fast for her taste. It was the same rush every lunatic she ever took down used before they attacked. Her shooting arm tensed and flexed toward her gun. She didn’t even realize it when her finger rested on the safety, gun gripped at the ready.

The bearded man reached their table and held on to the edge, shaking it slightly. “You people gonna arrest those Tyler bastards and their whore mother?” Even with her sitting down and out of line of his breath, Wallace could tell he’d been battling liquid demons most of day.

"Now why would we want to go and do a thing like that?" Shilling asked.

"Whatever happened up in them hills," he waved an unsteady finger at Shilling, "you can bet those Tylers had something to do with it!"

"Why do you say that?" Wallace asked. She returned her shooting hand to the table, reaching for her notepad.

"Because they killed my Katie!" he shouted.

The waitress scurried over. "I'm sorry, is this man bothering you?"

"No, it's fine. In fact, bring him some coffee." Wallace gestured to the chair across from her. "Please, have a seat."

The big man sagged into the chair and removed his cap. He slapped it down on the table hard enough to make their plates and glasses rattle.

"Lars Henrikkson." The waitress put a cup of coffee in front of him. Wallace noticed that seemed to calm him. She expected him to continue his verbal assault. Instead, he stared at the ripples in the surface of the steaming brew.

Wallace glanced at the customers around them, looking for any other surprises coming their way. Their table sat in the middle of the room, and while the murmur of the crowd continued, the people in the tables and booths nearest them had, for the most part, fallen silent. A couple beside them suddenly looked down at their food when Wallace caught them gawking.

"I don't know about you, Mr. Henrikkson, but I can use some air," Wallace said. "Would you like to step outside?"

Lars grumbled and grabbed his hat.

"Take care of the bill, Agent Shilling?"

"Will do." Her partner shot her a crooked smile and shook his head as he reached for his wallet.

"Gotcha again," she said with a wink. Sure, the Bureau would cover it as an expense, but now Shilling had to do all the paperwork.

Wallace picked up Lars's coffee and led him through the staring crowd to a door near the restrooms. It opened onto an enclosed porch running along one side of the restaurant. It was chilly. No wonder all the old geezers were inside, she thought. She invited Lars to have a seat on a bench near the corner and offered him his coffee as he sat down.

"So tell me about your Katie," she said.

Lars didn't bother to look at Wallace. It's as if at the touch of the warm mug, his gaze turned dark, his mind floating away. "My daughter worked for the Tylers waiting tables, cleaning cabins—general odd jobs they needed done. Then she started seeing their youngest boy, Will. After a time, I guess they fell in love, and he asked her to marry him. I hadn't seen her so happy since before her mother passed." A tear rolled down his cheek, carving a clean track through the grit and grime. He wiped it away, turning it into a long smear as his expression soured.

"Then they went to Vegas. I would like to have seen them get married proper, in a church, but neither of 'em have much family to speak of, so I gave her my blessing."

He stopped cold. Wallace lay a hand on his shoulder. His voice broke.

"Then he put a bullet in her head," he wailed. "She loved him so much, and he got her killed!"

"Are you saying Will Tyler shot your daughter?"

"I can't speak for who pulled the trigger, but sure enough her blood's on the Tylers' hands!"

"I've read the reports. They say a man named Marcus Rice killed your daughter and Will Tyler."

"I know all about the reports," Lars scowled. "They don't make a lick of sense. You don't think it's suspicious that nothing happened 'til Cole went down there? Either that sheriff is a bumbling idiot or he was in on it from the start! You got bodies burned before autopsies, missing murder weapons and bad investigations. There ain't a goddamn thing about my baby's death that looks right!"

"Let's back up a second, shall we?" Shilling came out to the porch. Wallace made a hurry-up motion and he shut the door. She pulled out her notebook. "Tell me more."

"It's like I said, there ain't much to tell, which is the problem. The coroner signed off on several death certificates, but there're no autopsies. Not one for Charles Rice, for Marcus Rice or even for Will Tyler. The Rice brothers were cremated and the Tylers declined an autopsy for Will. We had the local examiner take a look at Katie, but he couldn't tell me anything we didn't already know—that she was shot through the head and buried in quicklime. No gun was ever matched to the bullet in Will's head. They say Hess's deputy was killed with a knife, but no knife was ever found.

"You tell me, what evidence did they have to tie to Marcus Rice, who is conveniently dead and can't tell his own side of things? Isn't it funny that it's all wrapped up with a nice little bow after Cole Tyler goes down there to sort things out? I don't care if Will Tyler didn't pull the trigger on my little girl, but those Tylers are up to their necks in this thing!"

Wallace scrambled to keep up in her notebook. "Why was none of this in York's notes?"

"He did what he could, or so he said," Lars muttered.

"You didn't talk to anyone else about this?" Shilling asked.

"After my lawyer kept running into dead ends, we contacted the Nevada State Police, the state's attorney, even you people. Nothing seemed to happen after that. But you're payin' attention now, aren't you? Some lumberjack's daughter gets killed in the desert, nobody cares! But God forbid a couple tourists from the city get gunned down!" He pounded his fist on the arm of the bench. His coffee rattled across the surface. Wallace steadied it before it fell.

"Alright, Mr. Henrikkson, let's calm down," she said. "We're here to help."

"All I want is justice for my baby. I just miss her so much!" Lars started blubbering again.

"I think he's past coffee," Shilling said. "He needs to sleep this off."

"Yeah." Wallace read over her notes again. Whether Lars's claims were drunken ramblings or not, things with the Tylers were getting more and more interesting. If they had the juice to make bodies disappear in Nevada, they could feasibly be shipping just about anything to anywhere in the country from that airstrip.

"Uh-oh, you're getting that look," Shilling said. "What're you thinking?"

Wallace pulled her partner off the porch, far enough from Lars to get out of earshot. Not that he was in any shape to remember anything. "I'm getting us a warrant. We're going to search the Tyler grounds for any firearms that may match the bullets in the Paulsons' bodies."

"You think this Nevada business is related?"

"Maybe. But even if it isn't, it gives us a pattern of behavior. Combine that with Sean's history and I don't see how a judge would refuse it."

"I'll make some calls. You want Sheriff York and his men to back us up?"

"Yeah. Let's get a whole team in there. I don't know what the Tylers are hiding, but we're going to find out. I'm getting the feeling the Paulsons are just the tip of the iceberg."

NINETEEN

EMILY'S TITS EXCEEDED JEFF'S EXPECTATIONS. He laid her down across the sleeping bag and buried his face in them, swirling his tongue around her nipples and squeezing them in his hand. She cooed beneath him when he knelt between her legs and lined himself up.

"Put your hat on," she said.

"What?"

"Your cowboy hat! Put it on!"

"Whatever you say, ma'am." He'd certainly had—and fulfilled—stranger requests. So he leaned back and snatched it out from under his pile of clothes. He took his time putting it on, striking a dramatic pose as he did so.

"Oh God, that's so hot!"

"Damn straight." He worked the tip of his cock into her, then grabbed her ankle, thrust his hips to hers and buried himself to the balls. Even inside the dimly lit tent, he saw her eyes go wide when she let out a long moan. He grabbed her other ankle, stretched out those long legs, and started pumping. Slow at first, then faster and faster as he watched those tits bounce up to her neck.

Outside the tent, Hank finished a beer, crunched the can, and tossed it into the fire.

"I can't believe she's doing this." Jennifer sat mortified on the picnic table just a few feet away, her feet on the bench and elbows resting on her knees.

"People are funny sometimes." Hank reached into the cooler and fished out another beer. Devan or Dipshit or whatever his name was would just have to buy more if he got thirsty.

"It's not like the guys abandoned us, you know? They mean well."

"I'm sure they do." He'd been listening to this shit for the past fifteen minutes. She could make all the excuses she wanted for her friend, but it sounded more and more like jealousy to him. Now that she'd said her spell, maybe she'd finally wear down and let him get a little play.

"It could be a good opportunity for them, you know?"

"Man's gotta make a livin'." He slammed down half the beer.

"Yeah! I mean, what if the show takes off? Emily'd feel pretty shitty then, you know?"

If she said you know one more time, he just might punch her.

"I reckon so." He stood in front of her and set the beer down next to her.

"You didn't have to come along," she said. She sat up straighter. Even sitting on the table, she had to tilt her head up to look him in the eye.

"Didn't I?" She flinched as he set his hand on her knee, but she didn't move it away.

"N-no. I'm sure your friend will be okay."

"Who says I'm worried about him?"

Hank leaned in close and planted a kiss on her lips. She leaned away slightly, but her mouth opened when his tongue brushed her lip. Two seconds later, she relaxed and let him pull her closer.

Time to see what this fat girl can do, Hank thought. He broke off the kiss and unzipped his fly. She watched as he pulled out his dick. Those pretty eyes looked up into his, down at his crotch, then up again. He just stared at her expectantly, and after a moment she slid down to sit on the bench. Her hand was chilly and clammy, but she gave him a tentative squeeze that provoked a response. He could almost see the courage building up in her as she mouthed the head of his cock, then took it in a little further and stroked him, until at last she went to work in earnest.

She did a damn good job, too—lots of tongue, just enough teeth, and a strong rhythm. It felt so good Hank didn't hear the rustling in the bushes until the two men were on top of them.

"Who the hell are you?" the first guy demanded.

Jennifer released Hank and turned around, choking briefly. "Rick! Oh my God!"

Hank watched the guy storm across the site with his buddy close behind. Heading right for him while his limping jones swayed in the chilly night wind.

Rick stopped short of Hank. "What the fuck, Jen? Were you blowing this guy?"

Hank zipped himself up as he sized up the two guys. Rick looked to be about five-nine, with a stocky build hidden beneath his bulky flannel jacket. Hank couldn't quite tell if the meat under there was hard or soft. The other guy, who must be Devan, stood quite a bit taller than his buddy but didn't carry a lot of weight. He wore a worn leather bike jacket and a long, heavy wallet chain dangled halfway down his thigh. The guy at least wished he was hard, and a kick from those leather boots wouldn't feel good.

"Really, Rick, I didn't expect any of this to happen! We saw them at the restaurant, and—oh, shit, I'm sorry!"

"You fucking should be! I can't believe this!"

"Wait a minute." Devan grabbed his friend's shoulder. "Where's Emily?"

"Oh God!"

All eyes went to the tent as Emily squealed. "Oh! Oh! Oh! God. I'm . . . OHHHH!"

"That answer your question, partner?" Hank asked.

Devan scowled and charged toward the tent. Rick followed, brushing off Jen as she tried to stop him.

Hank rushed in to stand between them and the tent. "Whoah, you ain't goin' in there."

"Like hell I'm not! That's my fucking tent!"

"Yeah, and my friend's in there. The only way you're getting in is if you plan to hand him a towel."

Hank saw the punch coming a mile away, but he braced himself, clenched his jaw, and let it happen. Rick had a solid swing, even if he only connected with the last two knuckles. The blow put a nice sting on Hank's jaw. He liked feeling the pain. He grinned when he looked back at Rick before unleashing a left jab straight into Rick's nose, snapping the smaller man's head back.

Then it was on. Jennifer screamed as the three men traded blows. Devan grabbed a hold of Hank's right arm and tried to wrap it up in some kind of hold, but Hank shook him off with a side kick. It went low and struck Devan just below the hip, but it had the right effect and knocked him to the ground. Hank grabbed Rick's jacket and punched him once, twice in the face.

A solid blow struck the small of his back. Hank shouted in pain and fell to his knees. He looked up to see Devan gripping a hunk of firewood like a club. He raised it up over his head and Hank tried to get a hand up to intercept it.

Jeff, naked as the day he was born, but for his hat and socks, snatched the firewood right out of Devan's hand. Dumbfounded, Devan looked over his shoulder just in time to see Jeff's fist flying at his face. The punch snapped Devan's head around and he went down.

Rick swept his foot back and aimed a scoop kick at Hank's gut, but Hank caught it with both hands and twisted. Rick landed on his chest with a whumph, and two solid rabbit punches to his kidney took the fight out of him. He squirmed and screamed and clutched at his back.

Devan returned to his feet and put up his fists. Jeff slipped inside Devan's cross, put two quick punches into his gut and followed them up with an uppercut. Devan flopped onto his back next to his buddy. He held onto his face and groaned.

"Stop!" The guys turned to see Emily standing under the slit of the tent opening, holding a sleeping bag to her breasts. She hobbled over to Jeff and pounded on his arm with her fist. "Leave him alone!"

Jeff shoved her, sending her sprawling to the ground. The sleeping bag crumpled to her feet. Hank took a gander at her tits as she gawked up at the two of them in slack-jawed surprise.

"Are you crazy?" Jennifer knelt beside Emily and helped cover her up again with the sleeping bag.

"Fuckers!" Devan shouted. "You fuckers!"

"Hey, asshole, we were just doing what you neglected," Jeff said. "My girl had a rack like that, the last thing I'd be doing is chasing Bigfoot around!"

"Maybe they like hairy dudes," Hank ribbed.

"Oh, is that it? You into bears?"

"Just leave them alone!" Emily pleaded. Tears streamed down her face. Jennifer, showing off a nasty scowl, hugged her close to her chest.

"What're you crying about?" Jeff demanded. "Two minutes ago, you couldn't get enough!"

"Fuck you!" Devan sat up and touched his finger to his lip in search of blood.

Rick had stopped screaming. He crawled a few steps away and got a foot under him. As he started to stand, Hank stepped over and put a thrust kick into his ass. Rick dropped to his chest again. He turned around, but he got the picture and just came to a seated position.

"Cocksucker," Devan muttered.

"What was that?"

"You heard me! This is our campsite! Just get the fuck out of here, will you?"

"Uh-huh. Maybe you missed something here." Jeff grabbed a fistful of Devan's hair and yanked him closer. He held the guy's face about six inches from his now-flaccid penis. "The juices from your girlfriend's cunt are still drippin' off my dick, and I kicked your worthless ass! Now who's the cocksucker?"

He shoved Devan away and noted there was a tear in the man's eye. Devan scrambled back away from him. Hank laughed and picked up the rest of his beer.

"Whoo, that felt good!" Jeff shouted, grinning wide. "I'm gonna get my clothes."

"Before you boys get any ideas," Hank said, "you just remember who threw the first punches. Ask me, we did you boys a favor. These two broads, they didn't put up much of a fight. You take a look around you, note where we did our business. It ain't like we dragged 'em back to our place, you get me?"

Devan and Rick scowled at their girlfriends. The ladies just sniffled back their tears and hugged one another.

"You ready, Hank?" Jeff stood in front of the tent, now wearing his boots and jacket. He held the rest of his clothes in a bundle under his arm.

"Yeah. Let's get the fuck out of here."

"G'night, gents! It's been fun!" Jeff waved over his shoulder, as the two cowboys walked down the trail toward the main road.

TWENTY

THE RESTAURANT SIDE OF THE LODGE was empty, save for the waitress wiping down a table. She looked up when Rod came in.

"Evenin'!" she said. "Have a seat anywhere you like."

Rod sat down at a booth near the door. The waitress brought over a glass of water.

"Can I get you something to drink?"

"Coffee's fine. Is the kitchen still open?"

"They're cleaning up back there, but I'm sure we can rustle up something."

"Great. Listen, you wouldn't happen to have seen two big rednecks in here, would you?"

She chuckled. "I'm afraid you're going to have to be a little more specific. Most of our traffic is hunters, hikers, and campers."

“The two I'm looking for are built like linebackers, drink like fish, and like to wear these stupid-ass cowboy hats all the time.”

“Ahh, now we're getting somewhere. There were two guys with cowboy hats in here a little while ago.”

The tables and chairs all seemed intact, so they must not have gotten thrown out, he thought.

“Any idea where they went?”

“I don't know about where, but I can probably tell you what they're up to.”

“How's that?”

“They left with two ladies. They had a friendly chat in the corner, and next thing I know, they were headed out the door together.”

“Shit. Excuse me.” Rod slid out of the booth and past her.

“I thought you were hungry?”

“I just lost my appetite.”

TWENTY-ONE

"THAT'S THEM!"

Devan pointed at two big guys walking along the side of the trail. One of them wore no pants. Sean pulled the pickup onto the shoulder and rolled up behind them. When they turned around, it became obvious to Sean the pantsless guy wasn't wearing any underwear either. Tourists.

"Stay here," Sean said. He climbed out of the truck and approached the two men. They didn't look like the average college rowdies. Still, he didn't plan to treat them any differently from the rest of the drunken idiots they got at the lodge from time to time.

"Can we help you with something?" Hank demanded. He held up a hand to block the headlights.

"I was just going to ask you the same thing." Sean could feel the guy sizing him up. Each of these guys had a hundred pounds on him or more. He was lean and mean and had seen his fair share of scraps, but he had to play this one right or it could get ugly. He addressed the second guy. "How about it, fella? Someone steal your pants?"

Jeff grinned. "Just airing out the ole Texas longhorn, that's all!"

"Yeah? Looks more like a shortrib to me." Sean couldn't resist. He knew where this was headed. Might as well have fun while he played his part.

Hank guffawed. Jeff reached over and backhanded him across the arm.

"Listen, guys, I got a guy in the truck says you beat him up pretty good. Can you tell me anything about that?"

"Sure. They caught us bangin' their girlfriends and didn't take too kindly to it."

"Can you blame 'em?"

Jeff shrugged. "I suppose not."

"Where are you guys staying?"

"We got one of the cabins right up the road here."

"Alright, here's the deal. Obviously we can't have campers running around drinking and beating each other up."

"You throwing us out, Cochise?"

"Talking like that isn't going to help your case."

"Maybe you should ask your boy in there who drew first blood," Hank said. "The ladies invited us to their place. It's not like we went looking for a fight!"

"They're also not the ones walking around with their dicks flapping in the breeze."

"You got a problem with it?" Jeff dropped his clothes on the ground. "You going to do something about it?"

Hank grabbed his arm and pulled him back. He leaned in close and told him "Slow down. We get tossed, Rod'll kill us."

Jeff grunted and pulled his jacket closed. It just barely covered his groin.

"Are you finished or should we just bring in the authorities?" Sean asked. "Because I can tell you, Sheriff York and his deputies have no problem hauling drunks out of here for us."

"Fantastic!" Devan shouted through the truck window. "I'm pressing charges!"

"Hey, fuck you, dweeb!" Hank yelled. "We'll be happy to come over there and kick your ass again!"

The truck door flew open and Devan jumped out. "You can try!"

Ah, shit, Sean thought. He stepped in between Devan and the two rednecks before they could get to one another. It took all his strength to hold the two taller men apart. Jeff moved around the other side, also shouting threats. Right then, Sean wished he'd called Ronnie in for some extra backup after all.

A horn sounded up the road. Sean saw the two men in front of him relax almost instantly. He turned around to see a car zipping down the trail toward them. The horn honked rapid-fire until the car skidded to a halt near the truck. The driver, a black guy with a thin goatee, jumped out of the car. Sean wondered how things could get any more bizarre.

"What's going on?" The driver asked.

"Nothing we can't handle, boss," Jeff grumbled.

"You know these guys?" Sean asked him.

"They're with me, yes. They do something wrong?"

"You're Goddamn right they did!" Devan shouted. Then, pointing at Jeff, "This one banged my girlfriend, and then they—"

"Just let me handle this!" Sean broke in. He turned toward Rod. "It would appear your friends got caught with their hands in the cookie jar. Devan, here, took issue with that and a fight broke out. We're just now trying to get it sorted without involving the authorities."

"I'm sure it doesn't have to come to that," Rod said.

"Fuck you!" Devan shouted. "I'm pressing charges!"

Rod pulled out his wallet. "Come on, let's not be too rash. Tell you what. How about I pay for your campsite?"

Devan looked at Sean, who just shrugged at him. Sean didn't really care how things got resolved, so long as the problem went away fast. He expected belligerence from the rednecks. The driver, though, seemed calmer, sharper. Like most of the yuppies and corporate types that came through, he figured money would take care of anything he did wrong. Buying one's way out of trouble also saved the embarrassment of heading back home or back to work and having to tell family or a boss they got arrested for acting like an idiot. That saving of face mattered more than anything, but it didn't stop them from getting into trouble in the first place.

"How many days you staying? Two, three?"

"Four," Devan said. He watched Rod count through the bills in his pocket.

"Alright. Here, this ought to cover it and then some." He held up several bills. The headlights lit up Ben Franklin's portrait. Devan reached for them. But Rod snatched them back for a moment. "Provided, of course, there's no more talk of pressing charges."

Again, Devan looked to Sean.

"Your call, brother," Sean said. "Wasn't my girlfriend."

Devan frowned. He looked at the bills and then at Hank and Jeff.

"Going once . . ."

"Deal!" Devan took the bills and stuffed them in his pocket.

"If you're happy, I'm happy," Sean said. "Go ahead back in the truck while I have a talk with these guys."

Still scowling, Devan climbed into the truck and rolled the window back up.

Rod turned to Sean. “I'm sorry about this. I promise we won't cause any more trouble.”

It didn't surprise Sean that Devan backed off with the offer of money, but he did find it strange that the two big guys backed down so fast. Whoever this guy was, he was in charge.

“I should hope not. If one of my brothers had been here, you would all be out on your asses. We're no strangers to trouble. Everyone has their own idea of recreation, and we try not to get in the way. Sometimes, though, it interferes with the recreation of other campers, and we have to step in. If it happens again, we will have to ask you to leave.”

“You're being more than generous.” Rod took Sean's hand and shook it. “I apologize and, again, I promise you they won't cause you any more trouble.”

“Alright, then. You guys have a good night.”

“You too. Take care, now.”

Sean walked around the pickup and got in behind the wheel. Devan didn't say anything, he just stared daggers at the two big guys until Sean turned the truck around and headed back toward the campsite.

The speech didn't belong to Sean, it was an old one Cole liked to dust off from time to time. He wondered if Cole felt like such a tool when he delivered it.

TWENTY-TWO

ROD WAVED AS THE TRUCK PULLED AWAY. He was relieved he arrived when he did. Hank and Jeff would have made mincemeat out of that skinny punk kid. They wouldn't have given a second thought to his owning the place, and they'd be sitting in a cell waiting for the local cops to run their records.

Once the truck turned around the bend up the road, Rod turned to his two partners and kicked Jeff square in the nuts. Jeff let out a loud "woof" and collapsed to the ground, clutching at his groin.

"Jesus, Boss," Hank said. "Nice shot."

"Stand the fuck up!"

Wincing, Jeff sat up gingerly, then pushed himself to his feet.

"Are you two fuckin' stupid? I'm out there dealing with skinheads, and you go off dippin' your dicks and startin' fights! Are you trying to blow this deal? Do I need to remind you that our lives are on the line, here? If we don't deliver those guns, we are dead men—DEAD! You hear me?"

Jeff started the pleading. "C'mon, boss, we didn't set out to cause trouble. Those guys weren't supposed to be there."

"Do I look like I care about your fuckin' excuses?" he roared. "Stop thinking with your dicks! Now shut your motherfuckin' mouths and get in the motherfuckin' car!"

Rod was high with rage. He never lost his cool. Never. It's why he was hired by almost every outfit that mattered in the South. No matter what they thought about the color of his skin, he knew how to keep a deal together. But nothing about this deal smelled right, and he didn't need his sidekicks making it worse. The idea of driving up to Canada and disappearing appealed to Rod now more than ever. He had more than enough money to get started, but he knew he'd have to spend the rest of his life looking over his shoulder. Perhaps it was time to start giving serious thought to working alone. The less he had to rely on people, the fewer opportunities they had to let him down or land him in jail. Or worse—become Vargas's bitch forever.

Just twenty-four more hours, Rod told himself. Just hold it together for one more day and it'll be all over.

TWENTY-THREE

NINA HAD BEEN IN BED FOR HALF AN HOUR when the phone rang. She couldn't sleep anyway, so she grabbed the cordless phone off the nightstand.

"Hello?" Nobody answered, but Nina could hear breathing on the other side. She checked the caller ID to confirm her suspicion. "Please tell me you haven't been drinking again, Lars."

"What the fuck do you care?"

"You know I do."

"Bullshit."

The word stung. She cared for the man a great deal more than she could ever admit to him. The success of Will and Kate's relationship gave her hope, and she almost changed her mind. Then Kate died and Lars sought comfort in a bottle, and she realized she was too late.

"Why are you calling?"

" 'Cause I finally got you. I just spoke to the FBI."

Nina sat up. Her heart pounded.

"That's right," he said. "It's all over now. You and your bastard sons are finally gonna pay for what you done to my Katie."

"Lars, we didn't—" She held her tongue. It would do no good to argue, especially now. "What did you tell them?"

"That your son is a lying son of a bitch."

"Good night, Lars." She hung up.

With luck his drunkenness kept him from noticing the tremble that crept into her voice. Streams of moonlight flooded over her from the window that ran alongside her bed. Tears welled up in her eyes, and she wiped them away with the heel of her palm. She wanted to call him back and spill her guts. She wanted to come clean in hopes of restoring their previous relationship, and maybe bring Lars some closure.

She knew better. If she told Lars the truth, it would be all over for the Tylers. She lost Lars, and she suspected that even if Lars had known the full truth before Kate died in Nevada, the outcome would not have been any different.

It took another minute to get herself under control. She took one last deep breath, picked up the phone and called Cole's cell phone. He answered on the second ring.

"We've got a problem," she said.

TWENTY-FOUR

THE PLASTIC SHEETS and yellow crime scene tape sealing the plane's windows and doors snapped and popped in the night breeze, lit by the full white light of the moon. Cole loved that light. It made many things visible, plain as day, in the cold mountain darkness.

Flags marked the spots where forensics investigators found brass shell casings. Cole could just barely make out the pale circles of yellow spray paint surrounding bullets found in trees. Powdered chalk outlines indicated where Norman and Kara Paulson fell. Dark, glistening spots of blood were surrounded by each silhouette.

As thorough as the forensics teams tried to be with their cameras and chemicals, they did more harm than good. They trampled the grass, they ruined scents, and they made a mess of potential evidence on the trail with all their coming and going.

Cole crouched in the center of the clearing. Looking at the flags, he could see how one group could have been parked to his right. The other group could have come from the plane to his left. Then the Paulsons arrived from straight ahead, and the ground group opened fire. Norman went down. Someone shot the pilot. If the pilot stood by the plane when he got hit, then he hadn't been standing in a crossfire. Someone from the ground would have had to turn around to shoot him.

Unless Norman Paulson shot the pilot.

Intentional or blind luck? Shift Norman's barrel an inch to the right and he'd have missed the pilot by several feet. The bad guys on both sides could have mounted up and been gone before anyone knew what had happened, leaving two bodies and an unsolvable mystery.

He stepped to the edge of the strip and surveyed the scene again. If the FBI believed Cole and his brothers pulled the trigger, then they had to have a picture of the scenario before they could act on it. Cole needed to get in Wallace and Shilling's head. Especially Wallace. What would she see here?

Assuming they cleared the Paulsons, they probably went with the theory that Sean still grew marijuana somewhere on the property. Okay, so the pilot had a bundle of cash. Something went wrong—or perhaps they pulled a double-cross—and they shot the pilot and took home the cash and the crop.

Knowing it's all a load of horseshit, he recast the scenario. Someone met the plane. The Paulsons stumbled onto the meet and a firefight broke out. The pilot went down. The bad guys killed the Paulsons and bolted with everything.

Unless they weren't the only ones at the scene. Cole couldn't imagine a man coming into a deal solo, so the pilot must have had backup. He supposed they could have ridden out with the shooters, but it also made sense they could have survived the firefight and got out on foot. He'd never be able to tell which way in the darkness, but he also decided it would take a fool to run into the forest and just keep on running. If they had half a brain, they would return to the plane and explore their options. Maybe even follow the bad guys out. Trails led to roads. Roads led to towns, shelter, and phones. Trails meant the difference between survival and freezing to death in the wilderness.

Cole took a chance and turned on his flashlight. He walked down the trail, sweeping the beam back and forth across the tracks as he did so. The overgrown ruts indicated the trail had been unused for some time, but piles of branches he found along the side of the trail suggested someone had come through recently and cleared the way for the trucks. The grass had been flattened on the paths of the wheels. Yet, he found only one muddy patch in the first hundred feet. The tire tread could have belonged to the bad guys or the police.

He walked further down. He found another patch of mud. Then another. He almost walked past the second when he spotted a small depression off to one side. It looked like a boot print, smooth-soled with a pointed toe and tall heel.

Cowboy boots. Someone had walked out rather than driven out after all. Not a huge lead, but it was more than he started with.

Now he just had to convince the feds it meant something.

TWENTY-FIVE

THE WOLF DARTED through the trees, agitated.

He savored the feel of the cold air in his throat and lungs against the hot blood coursing through his chest. Rabbits darted out of his path. He smelled the trail of a doe, but hunger didn't drive him this evening. He ran, leaping over fallen trees and slipping through the rocks. He ran over the hills and across the valleys until he panted for breath and his tongue lolled out the side of his mouth. Then he ran some more.

He reached a small stream cutting through the hills. The moonlight caught the rhythmic dance between the water and the wind in shimmers that sparkled in the void of the primordial forest shadows. The stream came and went with the rains, but when it appeared, he always stopped for a drink of its clear water. He lapped it up and let the cold burn through his throat and settle into his belly. This was the way to live, reveling in the natural wonder of the world.

Then the wind shifted, and he smelled fire.

He followed the scent up the hill to the source, a campsite with four people arguing and bickering as they dismantled their tent. The two men wore fresh bruises on their faces, and the two women cried as they shouted at the men.

The wolf hated them already. They came to the woods for quiet enjoyment, but instead brought their car and generator noises and conflict with them. Their presence chased away game, spoiled scents, and marred the land, and now they couldn't even live with one another. These soft, noisy people stood at the top of the food chain?

One well-placed bite would change that.

This territory belonged to him. The predator. The alpha. Without their guns and their tools, what did they have? Just soft, weak flesh. They lived by his tolerance. If he walked into that campsite, they would scream in terror.

The wolf let a low growl rumble forth from its throat.

"What was that?" Emily froze and looked around, her eyes wide with a sudden heat of terror. The others froze. Listened.

If the wolf could laugh, he would. One little growl petrified them. He growled again and crept closer to the campsite.

"There it is again . . ." The brunette turned the other way.

"Is it a bear?" The blond tried to be rational, but her trembling voice gave her away.

The four of them dropped their gear and gathered near the fire. The men stood in front of the women to protect them, and the ladies' tears dried up, a stark contrast to their demeanor not thirty seconds ago.

Jennifer screamed and pointed at the dark figure at the edge of the tree line.

"What's that?" Devan asked. "Are those eyes?"

The wolf's eyes flashed in the firelight. He crept out of the shadows and moved closer toward them, his head lowered. He bared his teeth and let out a long snarl.

Both of the women screamed and clung to their boyfriends' backs. Rick backed away from the wolf and held his arms out wide to cover Jennifer.

"Beat it!" Devan shouted. He stomped the ground and shouted. Then he reached for a log of firewood.

The wolf barked and the man almost jumped. The four of them huddled together even more closely.

"Get to the car," Rick said. "We'll be safe in there."

The wolf advanced two more steps, growling and bristling. The humans continued to back away until they reached the car. Rick and Jennifer opened the driver's side doors. The wolf barked and jumped at them. They screamed and scrambled into the car, climbing over one another in their haste to get inside. Devan scrambled over the hood and jumped into the front passenger seat.

The wolf ran for the car as the doors slammed shut. He leapt onto the roof and scratched at the metal, barking and snarling the whole time. He jumped down to the trunk and snapped at the back window and reveled in the ladies' screams. He climbed over the roof and down to the hood, barking and scratching at the windshield. The two men pressed themselves into their seats and threw up their arms in protection. Devan honked the horn. He ran the windshield wipers. Wiper fluid sprayed across the glass and onto the roof.

"Start the car!" Emily screamed. "START THE CAR!"

"Who's got the keys?" Rick asked. The men patted and searched their pockets.

"I don't have them!"

"Neither do I! Fuck!"

"Beat it!" They shouted at the wolf. The women cried and held on to one another.

Satisfied, the wolf jumped off the hood. Moving toward the trees, he turned and barked at them one more time, and saw them flinch away from the windows again. Then he turned and trotted into the woods.

The wolf stopped at the edge of the darkness and turned back to watch the car for a moment. Then he sat to wait. He couldn't hear the humans anymore, but he could see movement inside.

How long would they wait? Minutes passed. Condensation started to appear on the interior of the car's windows. More time passed. At last, the wolf got bored and walked farther into the heart of the forest.

TWENTY-SIX

A LIGHT SNOW FELL as the darkness gave way to a dim, gray morning. There were enough obstacles in this case. Wallace didn't need the cold and wetness of snow to make things worse, but that's how cases always turned. Always conspiring, never fast and easy like she wanted.

Standing beside Shilling, she pulled on a pair of white rubber gloves and watched York and his deputies standing together. They sipped coffee out of foam cups. Tufts of gray hair stuck out from the back of one deputy's cap, and his belly stretched his jacket to its limit. The other three deputies were younger, possibly fresh out of school or the academy and willing to take any job that would get their training paid for. Young and cocky, they seemed the type who would move on as soon as a posting in a bigger department opened up. If someone needed to justify cop stereotypes, this was a picture-perfect moment.

"Sheriff York, may I have a word?" she asked, hiding her disgust.

"Of course." York left his men to stand beside her.

"Are you and your men okay with this search?"

"Pardon?"

"If any of them are friendly with the Tylers, tell me now."

"Ah, I see. Don't worry, ma'am. Some of the fellas have hunted this land—myself included—but they'll do this right."

"Good. Show me again where we're going."

Sheriff York nodded at both Wallace and Shilling. He rubbed his hands together for a moment, then put one hand in his jacket and the other outward before him. His breath was visible in the increasingly cold morning. "The Lodge itself is the restaurant and offices. On the other side is the garage and tool shed. Farther back in the trees is the Tyler house, their main residence."

"Do all the Tylers live there? Mom and the siblings?"

"It's possible. They have a lot of cabins, though, so I can't speak for where the boys live."

"Agent Shilling, get into their registration system. Any cabin we can't verify as being rented out to a visitor, we search."

"Sounds like a plan."

"Let's do this." Wallace turned to address the whole group. "We're searching for the potential murder weapon in the Paulsons' death, specifically any rifle chambered for a .223 caliber. I'll take firearms, ammunition, magazines and anything else that even hints at the existence of such a weapon! If you find anything of interest, alert me or Agent Shilling immediately. If any member of the Tyler family interferes with your search, put the cuffs on them. Any questions?"

The deputies stood silent with cups in hand, steam floating, snow falling.

"Then here we go!"

Shilling took a deputy to the lodge while York and the older deputy headed for the garage. Wallace led the last two across the field to the house.

The house itself sat back in the forest behind a cluster of trees, affording the family some privacy from the main operation of the campground. Constructed of logs like the lodge, it had one main floor. The windows in the foundation indicated a basement level. Smoke curled up from a stone chimney on one side of the house. Lights glowed in two windows nearby. A concrete walk led up to a covered porch.

The front door opened as Wallace and the deputies approached. Nina Tyler stepped outside. She wore a loose sweater with jeans and hiking boots and she had her hair tied back into a ponytail. She sipped from a steaming mug of coffee, then smiled.

"Good morning, Agent Wallace, gentlemen. What can I do for you?"

"We have a warrant to search the premises." Wallace held out the paper.

"Oh my. I guess you better come in then." Nina ignored the warrant and stood aside.

Wallace and the deputies stepped inside. The tidy living room boasted a sparse, rustic décor with its polished wood paneling and vaulted ceiling, yet the family photos on the walls indicated a mother's touch. A red throw rug with a jagged yellow design along the border dominated the center of the room. The fire filled the room with heat and amber light. More pictures and a clock flanked by statuettes of Indians riding horses stood on the mantel. The only truly modern amenities were the flat-screen television hanging on the opposite wall from which a cable ran down to a rack of electronics flanked by two large speakers and a subwoofer.

"Can I help you find anything?" Nina asked.

"We'll help ourselves, thanks." Wallace directed the deputies to a door and a hallway off the main living area.

"Suit yourselves."

"Where are your sons, Mrs. Tyler?"

"They're already working. But don't worry, they won't get in the way."

"I see." A family picture caught Wallace's eye, and she recognized the teenaged versions of Ronnie and Cole. Of the other two boys, she wondered which was Sean and which was Will. A pretty girl knelt on the ground in front of Nina. They looked happy, just like any other family, though there was no sign of their father. She wondered if he had taken the picture or if he had already died by the time it was taken. "May I ask how you knew we were coming?"

"I got a phone call from Lars Henrikkson last night."

Wallace winced. She should have had him dropped in the drunk tank.

"He told me you spoke and that you'd be by to arrest us all."

"You have to admit the circumstances surrounding your son's death are suspicious."

"So they keep telling me."

Wallace walked through the kitchen and opened a few cabinets. It didn't make sense that Henrikkson would call to warn her, so he must have been gloating. She remembered he had called Nina a whore. Another possible motive sprung up in her mind.

"How long were you dating Lars Henrikkson?" she asked.

"Oh, it never got that far," Nina said.

"But he wanted it to."

"For a time. Lars was a sweet man. But he took it hard when his wife died. He hunted here quite a bit, so I knew him well enough. As a widow myself, I helped him through his grief. I suppose it was only natural."

"You broke his heart, is that it?"

"He understood. It's just not the relationship I was looking for."

"How did his wife die?"

"A car accident. She was struck by a drunk driver coming around a blind curve. Killed her instantly. This was back in . . . '01? No, '02, a little before deer season."

"I see. And now he's using us to get even with you, is that it?"

"I'm afraid it's not that simple," Nina said. Wallace couldn't read her yet, which frustrated her. If it were a stupid gang punk, she'd already know if he was lying, what he was hiding and why.

Nina took another sip from her mug. "Lars isn't petty. He's legitimately angry over Katie's death. It affected us all, to be sure, but Lars really does blame us for her death."

"Yet this doesn't bother you?" Wallace returned to the living room, "This intrusion into your lives?"

"We welcome strangers into our home every day, Agent Wallace."

"I can't imagine they rifle through your personal belongings."

A shrug. "When you have nothing to hide, what does it matter?"

"I find that hard to believe, Mrs. Tyler."

"That I'm not upset you're here?"

"That you have nothing to hide."

"I guess you'll find out."

"You're damn right I will." Wallace stepped in close to Nina and towered over her. "Then you'll be upset, won't you?"

"Don't you worry about that, Agent Wallace. When the time comes, a mother knows how to defend her family." Nina's eyes narrowed for half a second, then that sweet expression returned. "Can I get you some coffee?"

TWENTY-SEVEN

"CAN WE TALK?"

"Oh, hey Cole." Caught off guard, Sheriff York stood up quickly, closing Ronnie's Snap-On tool chest as he straightened from his slouch to look up. Cole sensed York was embarrassed. It was more than his look—reddening cheeks, shifty eyes—like a boy who has been caught rummaging through his old man's porn stash. "Uh, yeah, we can talk."

"I need your help."

"With?"

"C'mon, Pat, you know what I'm asking."

"I suppose I do." York checked on his deputy just outside of the garage searching the vehicles. He probably wouldn't hear them, but just the same, York leaned in close to Cole and lowered his voice. "I gotta tell ya, Cole, this woman has a real hair up her ass about Nevada. In fact, that's what helped her get this warrant."

"That's why I need to talk to you."

York looked up at Cole, looking for his eyes. To read them. "Are you ready to come clean about what happened there?"

Cole didn't respond.

"That's what I was afraid of. You're going to have to give me the whole story if you want help."

"Fair enough, Sheriff."

Cole turned his back on York and walked away. He could almost feel the sheriff watching him go.

York finally snapped. "Damn it, Cole. What have you got?

Cole stopped and turned to face him. "I went out to the crime scene last night."

He gave Cole a frustrated look. Cole half expected York to give him a chewing out for interfering with an investigation or spoiling evidence.

"And?"

"I found a bootprint a little ways down the trail," Cole said. "I think someone survived the gunfight and walked out of there."

"You're sure it's not one of my guys?"

"Any of them wear cowboy boots?"

"I don't think so. We get duty boots for the department. You're sure it's a fresh print? That it couldn't have been left a few days back?"

"You know I can track better than that."

"I suppose you can. Alright, I'll tell you what. Let her get this search out of her system and I'll talk to her about this bootprint. I want your word, though, Cole! Tell me you and your brothers don't have anything to do with this!"

"I swear it, Pat. On my father's grave."

York scowled as he mulled that over. He knew Cole didn't make that promise lightly.

"I guess that'll work."

"Thanks, Pat. I appreciate it."

"Don't thank me yet. One of these days, you and I are going to sit down and have a chat about Nevada. Everybody's entitled to their secrets, but just remember: those secrets often come back and bite us in the ass."

"And then some," Cole muttered.

TWENTY-EIGHT

RONNIE FOUND THE CAMPSITE in total disarray. The tent had collapsed, trash still lay strewn around the ground, and an array of tools and gadgets surrounded a pair of backpacks on the picnic table. Frost covered the car windows and the fire had died down to just a small cluster of embers releasing a thin tendril of smoke. A fine dusting of snow fell across it all.

He walked around the site, but found no sign of the four campers. No recent footprints anywhere. The collapsed tent appeared to have been emptied and dismantled, though the job hadn't been finished. He returned to the car and scraped a bit of frost off the window. When he tried to peer through the gap, he realized the interior of the window had fogged over. He gave the window four sharp knocks.

A moment later the car shifted on its suspension. Someone spoke inside, but the car muffled their voice. The door opened and a blonde girl rubbed her eyes as she looked up at Ronnie.

"Good morning," he said. "You guys okay?"

She looked at Ronnie, visibly disoriented. She looked around the campsite, then up at the sky.

"I guess we are now." She leaned back into the car. "C'mon, guys. It's morning."

One by one the other doors opened. Another girl and two guys climbed out. They stretched sore backs and worked the kinks out of their joints.

"Did you guys spend the night in the car?"

The blonde nodded up at Ronnie. He stood well over her. His eyes couldn't help run down past her eyes and chin, down to her cleavage. But he caught himself when one of the guys moved toward him.

"We were packing up early," Devan said. "Then this wolf attacked us!"

"Attacked? Were you bitten?"

"We got in the car before it could try."

"Don't tell me you spent all night in there . . ."

"Yup," Emily said. "Longest night of my life! I gotta pee so bad!"

"Why didn't you call someone?"

"We honked the horn, but nobody came." Devan shrugged. "After a while I didn't want to waste the battery.

Meanwhile, the keys and phones are all on the table. I was going to take an inventory before we packed up."

"Wow. I'm sorry, folks. I wish I'd stopped by a few hours earlier, but things have been pretty crazy this week. Is there anything I can do for you?"

"No, thanks. We just want to get on the road and get home. I think we've all had enough adventure for now."

"Damn right," Rick said. "I'm gonna go behind that tree and piss, then I'm going to stuff everything in the trunk and get the fuck outta here. You can keep this nature shit, dude. I'm done!"

Ronnie stuck around for a few minutes longer and did his best to provide good customer service. He asked that they at least stop by the lodge for some free coffee to keep them awake on their travels. They weren't interested. Ronnie left them alone as they scrambled in a flurry of pointless activity, gathering camping gear he was sure they would never use again. He returned to his truck.

As he left the campsite this time, he laughed long and hard.

TWENTY-NINE

SHIT!

When he saw the police cruisers parked near the lodge, Rod stopped the car cold on the gravel road. They were far enough away that their presence was obscured by a tree line that led to the entrance. Rod could see the lodge sign and driveway far off to his right. There were no officers near the front, which meant they were deep in the grounds looking for something. Rod felt a shiver on the back of his neck. Did he miss something? Did the nazi fucks leave any weapons at the airstrip? Rod let the car engine idle and his mind wander thinking of the angles to the situation.

Then Jeff, sitting with Rod in the front seat, saw them. "We're screwed."

Rod wasn't convinced.

Then Hank rushed to peek his head out from behind Jeff's seat, slipping his mug between both of them in the front. "Are you kidding, boss? Drive us the hell out of here while you still can!"

"Think about it for a second! If they were here for us, they'd have arrested us already." Rod paused to consider the gambit. "Here, let's find out."

Rod rolled down the window and flagged down a car coming their direction. The driver rolled down the window.

"Mornin'!" Rod said, smiling that Mayberry smile and nod the locals on this trip seemed to favor. "Do you know what's going on in there?"

"It looked like a search to me," the other driver said. "Kinda weird. I'm wondering if we shouldn't pack up and leave."

"A search? For what?"

"Beats me, man. I'm guessing it's something to do with that business with the airplane."

Shit! "Oh, yeah, I heard about that." The angles and possible outcomes began to rush through his mind. "Listen, are they still serving breakfast? Or are they shut down?"

"Sure, at least eggs and toast, I think."

"Thanks! I'm starving!" And with that, Rod waived and smiled again, leaning back in the car. The other car pulled past.

Rod kept his foot on the brake as he rolled his window back up. He smiled, though this time, it wasn't so wide, and his eyes were narrower. The angles were coming into sharper focus. "See that? Perfect!"

"What, breakfast?"

"No, shithead! The cops! Obviously, they're checking into the lodge owners. If they're searching the place, they've probably got a warrant. If they've got a warrant, then these people are the prime suspects."

Rod drummed on the steering wheel for a moment. It actually made sense. These people lived right here, giving them opportunity. A hunting lodge would have guns on the premises, so a search could easily turn up the means. It didn't matter that they wouldn't find the real murder weapon because they could spend all day waiting on ballistics and searching for a motive. By the time they cleared these people, he and the guys would be long gone. He checked the mirror, then turned the car around and headed back to the cabin. He might not need to travel north after all.

"We're not getting breakfast, then?" Hank asked.

"Just shut up."

THIRTY

"WE JUST WASTED OUR TIME." Wallace hurled her rubber gloves into the trunk.

The search consumed over two hours. Shilling came around and lowered the two .223-caliber varmint-hunting rifles they found into the trunk. They found both in a small gun safe in the Tylers' basement. None of the other firearms were anything spectacular. The collection, as a whole, was much smaller than she expected from a family running a hunting lodge. While either of the two rifles could have punched holes in the Paulsons, neither had the threatening look that told other criminals the bearers meant business.

"I'm not going to disagree," Shilling said as he shut the trunk.

"If they knew we were coming, the real murder weapon could be buried in the forest. We could search for years and never find it!" Wallace was pissed. Her anger was aimed at that old drunk, Lars Henrikkson.

"Yep."

"And Mom's attitude, that just burns my ass! It's like she knew she had us!"

"Mm-hmm."

"No, really, Brian, the pep talk's completely unnecessary! I know you want to pump me up, but let's not take it too far!"

"Sorry, Ange," he said with a smile. "I'm just trying to figure out our next steps."

She spotted Cole and Sean standing near the lodge building. Cole wore a leather motorcycle jacket that hung open despite the cold. Sean wore a padded denim vest over a hooded sweatshirt. He wore his hair short and spiked. To Wallace, their outward appearance couldn't be any more different. But they're blood, she thought. At the end they're the same. They spoke to one another until Cole noticed her looking his way. When he nodded toward Wallace, Sean turned her way. Cole held eye contact with her, his expression was as stoic as ever. Sean laughed at some joke of his own, then raised a fist and extended his middle finger. They're blood and they have blood on their hands. She just can't prove it yet.

Cole slapped him on the back of the head.

"Come with me." Wallace walked toward the squabbling brothers.

"What are we doing, Ange?" Shilling asked.

"We're just going to have a chat, that's all."

Sean grinned until Cole said something to him. Wallace couldn't make out the words, but Sean turned to argue.

"I said get lost!"

Wallace heard that one just fine. Sean didn't put up any more fight after that. He just scowled and slunk away around the side of the building toward the garage.

"You guys having a good time?" she asked Cole.

"You'll have to excuse my brother. He doesn't always think before he acts."

"Does he have a problem with our search? I thought you had nothing to hide?"

"Nobody's going to be happy if you take away the hunting rifle their father gave them before he died."

"How's he going to feel when we match one of those rifles to the Paulson bullets?"

"You won't."

"I guess you made sure of that, didn't you?"

Cole shook his head.

"It worked in Nevada, right? I'll bet it gets easier every time."

"Are you about done, Agent Wallace? I've got work to do, and I imagine you do as well."

"You don't worry about me, Mr. Tyler. I'm not going anywhere."

"Suit yourself. I just hope the real killer doesn't walk because you're too busy chasing ghosts." Cole pushed between them. "Excuse me." Then he went back into the lodge.

"You're going to enjoy taking him down, aren't you?" Shilling asked.

Wallace frowned. The Paulsons came up clear. The Ervins went home and went back to their day jobs, and nothing unusual came up on Carter. She'd do her due diligence and speak to both brothers. She'd chase down any leads that came from the property search. But her gut insisted Cole and the rest of the Tyler clan wanted them out of their lives for a reason.

That wouldn't happen any time soon. Even if they had no connection to the Paulsons, she vowed to look into the Nevada problem. If they did have something to hide, she would find it.

"You bet your ass I'm going to enjoy this," she told Shilling.

THIRTY-ONE

ROD LOOKED OUT THE FOGGING WINDOW from inside their cabin. He watched the falling snow. He had only seen snow a few times in his life, and he wondered if it always snowed this early in the season this far north. Most of the time he read about snow, people described it as beautiful and sparkling, and talked up its clean purity and sharp white color.

Not today. The snow draped the world in mottled gray. The leaves on the trees had turned and many had fallen, leaving black, skeletal fingers grasping toward the sky. He appreciated the bright colors of the trees that did retain their leaves. But he may as well have been viewing them through a layer of static, as if watching a television show after a younger brother bumped the rabbit ears out of place.

He worried the snow might interfere with the trade tonight. If his guys couldn't get through or the skinheads didn't show, it would be all over. Vargas would mount their skulls to the wall.

The TV weatherman, however, assured him the accumulation would be limited. Even now, he could see campers driving back and forth along the trails with no effort or even any real reduction in speed. Surely the locals knew how to keep their roads clear, too. They certainly had enough experience.

Worst case, if he could slog through five feet of Katrina flood waters to find food and shelter, he could damn well make it through a couple inches of snow. His life depended on it now as much as it did then. These racist pinheads had nothing on the cartel. Spouting rhetoric and dragging teenagers behind cars put a scare into people, but Vargas and the men he worked for fought the police and the military on both sides of the border. The cartel put their money into training, resupply, and keeping business moving rather than pissing it away on hookers and crank.

If a man played his cards right, money always generated more money. Users and losers would never understand that; their money always went straight to the player.

"What's the game plan, boss?" Hank asked from the edge of the bed.

"Get your coats on, guys. We're going for a walk."

"Where to?"

"Out to the meet site. We're supposed to be hikers, and that's what we're going to look like. Meanwhile, we're not going to let those shitheads get the drop on us. One way or another, we're leaving with our goddamn guns."

THIRTY-TWO

COLE AND SEAN SAT IN THE BACK OFFICE and scarfed down a quick lunch of cheeseburgers and chicken fingers. The morning cook took one look at the police and turned around and went home, so Cole spent the morning manning the grill. Now he sat down to see what other damage had been done by the feds.

"The fallout hasn't been too bad, considering." He took one more count off the guest register printout. "Only four early checkouts. That frees up one cabin and sites eight, fifteen, and twenty-four."

"Twenty-four was those four college kids, wasn't it?"

"Yeah, that's right."

"Oh, man," Sean said with a laugh. "I'm not sure they left because of the cops."

"What happened?"

"A couple of shitkickers kicked the shit out of them. I was doing the rounds last night and found them all arguing. One of the guys said these other two guys nailed their girlfriends and then beat 'em up."

"Nice. Did you handle it?"

"It gets better! I took one of them to find the guys, and we found them walking back to their cabin. One of them hadn't even gotten dressed! He was wearing nothing but his jacket and his boots! Said he was just 'airing out his Texas longhorn!' "

Cole's head snapped around. If the plane was from Houston . . .

"I tell you, I haven't seen anything like that since—"

"Wait a minute, you said boots. Cowboy boots?"

"Yeah, that's right. Why?"

"Shit! You said they were staying in a cabin. Which one?"

"Beats me." Sean shrugged.

"Think, Sean! Which one?"

"I said I don't know! What's the big deal?"

"They may be the killers the feds are looking for! Do you remember anything else?"

"Yeah, there was a black dude with them. He stopped and picked them up before another fight broke out."

Cole scanned the guest register with his finger. He found three men had checked in under the name Harold Carter the night of the killings.

"Go get Ma," he said.

"I'll get Ronnie, too. We can take these guys! We'll tie 'em up in a little bow and let Pat come clean it up! Those feds'll be outta here by nightfall!"

"No! Don't tell Ronnie yet. Just get Ma! We'll decide from there."

"Alright, alright! I'll be right back." Sean ran out of the office.

Cole grabbed the mouse and clicked on the Address Book icon on the computer screen. A couple more clicks and he had Pat's entry and his cell phone number.

Sean returned with Nina a moment later.

"Did Carter and his guys have a reservation?" Cole asked.

"No. Sean says you think they're the killers?"

"I found a print from a cowboy boot on the trail out of there. Did they have a car?"

"No idea. But I do remember their boots clattering on the floor."

"Good enough. I'm going to call Pat."

"No, wait a second." Nina opened the desk drawer and pulled out a business card. She handed it to Cole. "Call Agent Wallace."

"Are you kidding?" Sean asked. "She's not going to listen to us!"

Cole looked at the card, then reached for the phone. Sean did have a point. The woman was just as likely to arrest them as these other guys.

"You sure about this, Ma?" Cole asked. "I talked to Pat earlier, and he's willing to give us a hand with this."

"No, go straight to the source," Nina said. "Call Agent Wallace."

Cole dialed the cell phone number listed on the card. Mom's instinct never steered them wrong.

THIRTY-THREE

THE FIRST THING WALLACE CAUGHT after Shilling parked next to Harold Carter's car were the plates: they were dealer issue. Why would a man from Reno have a dealer car in Minnesota?

According to Cole, the cabin Mr. Carter rented was among the smaller ones on the property, consisting of one large bedroom and living area with a small kitchenette and a full bathroom. The record showed three men had registered.

They waited in the car, taking stock of the perimeter. A large propane tank stood near the back corner, and a small stoop butted up to the front door. The grounds didn't seem disturbed as she expected. No evidence of a campfire, beer cans, cigarette butts. Tidy cabin grounds is not what she'd expect from three men in the wild. Something wasn't right with Mr. Carter and friends.

"You best not be yanking our chains here," Wallace told Cole as she turned to stare him down in the back seat.

"Don't worry, Agent Wallace," Cole said. "I don't do bullshit."

Shilling smirked at that, but got back to serious when he saw Wallace turned back to face the front of the cabin.

"You've got the key?"

Cole handed it to Shilling who drew back his arm to grab it.

"Stay here. And stay out of the way."

Wallace and Shilling didn't bother to close their doors. They drew their pistols as they approached the front door. Before reaching the steps, she looked back to see if Sheriff York and his men were ready. They parked behind the Taurus, in a half circle around the cabin. The deputies stood braced against their cars, aiming their shotguns at the front windows and door of the cabin. Cole had gotten out of the car and stood beside York.

Wallace reached the door and moved to right side of the frame, her gun held low. Shilling positioned himself on the left side. He nodded to her. She knocked on the door.

"Federal agents, Mr. Carter! Open the door!"

No response. No sound of movement inside.

She pounded on the door again, then slid the key into the lock and turned it. Still no rustling inside. She looked at Shilling and counted off a silent "one, two, three" then threw the door open. It slammed against the inside wall with a loud clack and bounced back into Shilling as he rushed in after Wallace.

They lead with their guns. Wallace swept hers across the room, scanning the beds and the open closet, the pile of clothes near the television and the table and chairs in the corner. She and Shilling converged on the bathroom together. Shilling went in first, checked the room, then relaxed and holstered his pistol.

"We're clear," he said.

Wallace went outside and waved off the deputies. York handed off his shotgun and he and Cole walked up to Wallace.

"Any idea where they could be?" she asked York.

Cole shook his head. "When they signed in, they claimed they were here to do some hiking. They could be anywhere in the forest, really."

"Call in the dealer plates, would you Sheriff?"

"Already did. Looks like they belong to Daly Dodge in town," York said. "They sometimes rent out their cars. I'll give them a call and see who rented it."

"Thank you."

Wallace went back into the cabin. She and Shilling poked through what little they found. Fast food and junk food wrappers filled the trash can. Beneath the food wrappers, she found a handful of clothing tags, complete with prices. Receipt from a thrift shop and a grocery store listed several clothing items, toiletries and a coat. The buyer paid in cash only a day ago.

“Brian, look at this.” She handed over the receipts.

Sheriff York ran into the cabin as they looked it over.

“The car was rented just yesterday,” he said. “Unfortunately, the service guy checked it out to a Dick Hertz.”

“Well, that's helpful,” Wallace said.

It didn't make sense to her. Carter and his men should have rented that car and headed straight for home. The only reason she could figure for them to stick around was if they weren’t here for the hiking at all. Maybe Mr. Carter and his boys were here to make a deal. Maybe they needed to make the deal that went south at the airstrip. But why here? Had the Tylers brokered the deal? The county records showed the land was tied up in someone's estate. If the Tylers were familiar with the land, they would know nobody was using it. Yet, if they had brokered the deal, it would be suicide to give up their partners to the authorities.

Unless they were already buried out in the woods somewhere, she thought. There are worse ways to hide a deal gone wrong, and launching a missing persons search or an APB for Carter would tie up a lot of time and resources, not to mention divert her attention from the Tylers.

Cole stood in the doorway, his expression flat. It bothered the hell out of Wallace more than ever that she couldn't read him.

"Mr. Tyler, I would like you and your family to get the word out to your customers to be careful and not approach anyone." She paused as a new thought struck her. "Even better, get them back to your lodge and keep them there."

"Yes, ma'am." Cole pulled a cell phone out of his pocket and went back outside.

"We need to find these guys. Sheriff, send one of your men back out to the airstrip. The rest of us will fan out and start looking for tracks out here. They couldn't have gotten far on foot. Whoever finds them, we call it in and wait for backup."

"Shouldn't we use one of the Tylers for the search?" York asked. "They know this land better than anyone else."

"Not just yet. I'm still not convinced they're clear of this."

"C'mon, lady. They called us in for Christ's sake, and we've got three men we can put at the scene. What more proof do you need?"

"You want your friends off the hook? Then get your ass out there and find me Harold Carter and the other two men! This morning you assured me your friendship with the Tylers would not interfere with this investigation. Is that not still the case?"

York's lip curled into a snarl, and for a moment there Wallace thought he would fire back at her. She wanted him to lose it; she was convinced a secret would come out.

"We'll do our jobs," he said evenly.

"Thank you!" She addressed the deputies that had stopped in their tracks to watch the showdown. "Now get out there and lets find these pieces of shit before someone else gets killed!"

THIRTY-FOUR

ROD STOOD AS THE TWO BLACK SUVS ROLLED into the valley. The glare across their windshields and their blacked-out side windows made it impossible to see inside. The drivers took their time and maneuvered through the trees, which made him feel a little better because feds would have charged right in and arrested them. He supposed the skinheads could have traded in their pickups for new wheels, or maybe kicked the deal up their chain of command, but he hoped it was his backup plan that had arrived.

Beside him, Jeff reached into his jacket and unsnapped the catch on his shoulder holster.

"Don't get too crazy," Rod whispered. "They may be on our side."

The SUVs stopped just a few feet away from him. He could see the men in the front seat at last: two twenty-something black kids wearing heavy winter coats and knit caps. The driver must have weighed three hundred pounds, easy. They traded glares with Hank and Jeff. Rod ignored them and went around to the passenger side of the second SUV. A tall, chunky black man climbed out and slammed the door shut. The guy's smile was so tall and wide, it split his round face in two when he spotted Rod. They gave one another a quick embrace.

"Thanks for coming, Trey," Rod said. "I appreciate it."

"Hey, it's all good, brother! I owed you one. Not to mention that paycheck you mentioned. That's still on the table, right?"

"Of course!"

"My man! This your crew?"

"Yeah. Trey, meet Hank and Jeff."

" 'Sup, gents?"

"How you doin'?" Jeff said. Hank nodded.

"Trey and I go back a ways."

An understatement at best. Rod and Trey ran together in high school, pulling minor jobs and doing their best to stay ahead of the pigs. They later found their own niches and went their own way, but continued to back up one another when needed. Rod stepped up in a big way after Katrina, putting Trey up in a new place in Houston and helping him establish the contacts he needed to get his feet under him again.

"What happened that you needed us way the fuck up here?" Trey asked.

"Long story," Rod said. "Did you guys bring the ordnance?"

"Of course! Trey always delivers, baby!"

"Alright, this is what we're going to do. Our dealers are coming in the same way you did. They'll be loaded for bear, so I want two men up on these two ridges." Rod pointed up the hill on either side of the valley. "If shit goes sideways, I want you to cut the fuckers down. These guys are already going to be on edge, and it's not going to take much to set them off. If we have to leave behind some dead nazi trash, then so be it."

"Why not do that anyway? Just kill 'em all and walk away with the guns and the money? Wipin' out skinheads, seems to me, you'd be doing our country a favor."

"Because we got feds in the house."

"What? You didn't say nothin' 'bout no G-men!"

"It's cool, Trey, trust me! We just need to do this and get gone. If we leave a trail of bodies behind, they'll never let it go."

Rod saw Trey wavering. Their friendship was thicker than blood, but the feds spooked him good. Always had. Then Trey said what Rod already knew was coming: "I don't know, man."

"Have I ever steered you wrong?"

Trey cocked an eye at him.

"Alright, aside from that one time. How was I supposed to know she had a prosthetic leg?"

"It was kinda hard to miss once I got her pants off. Yeesh!"

"Didn't stop you though, did it?" Rod clapped him on the shoulder.

"Hey, pussy's pussy!"

"And a paycheck's a paycheck. C'mon, let's get to work."

Trey introduced the rest of his crew while they started setting up. The two kids from the first SUV were just driving partners and muscle. Rod was more interested in meeting Mo and Darryl, his insurance policies for the evening. Mo had pocked, dark skin on his face, and deep-set eyes that stared right through Rod. With his gaunt features, he looked like he'd just stepped off a boat from Africa. Darryl, on the other hand, looked like any other homeboy off the hood in any parish back home, but with a casual demeanor as he shook Rod's hand. They broke out their gear and discussed their plans. But Rod noticed Hank and Jeff stood at bay, away from the new crew. He didn't need this shit now.

Rod pulled Hank and Jeff together.

"You guys good with this?"

"Yeah, Boss," Jeff said. "We're with you."

Hank held up a hand. “I just have one question.”

“Yeah?”

“How'd that work with the prosthetic leg? Seems to me, you mount up doggie style, you're going to keep falling over to one side.”

Rod glared at him a moment, then shook his head and walked away. “I’ll diagram it for you someday.”

They were in. The plan was falling into place.

THIRTY-FIVE

NINA PULLED COLE INTO THE OFFICE and closed the door behind them. The order from agent Wallace to sequester the lodge guests unnerved her. Never mind the potential public relations fallout if the media caught wind of it; the situation was escalating. Attention is the last thing she wanted.

"How are we doing?" she asked.

"Not bad," Cole said. "We've got most of the campers accounted for. Some came back here to the lodge, and I've got the cooks making up some sandwiches and coffee to keep them quiet. A few others agreed to be careful or locked themselves in their cabins. There are only a couple we couldn't account for, so I'm guessing they must be out hiking already."

"Not much we can do about that now. Any sign of the feds or Pat's men?"

"Sean spotted them cruising Pine Ridge Road—said they never even got out of their car."

"Shit." Nina dropped down into the chair in front of the desk. "Between the snow and the trees, they're not going to spot anything from the road! Are they at least watching the cabin?"

"They're having the rental car towed and one of the deputies stayed behind."

"So they don't even have their full manpower. I wonder if we shouldn't be out there helping them anyway. The sooner we can make this go away, the better."

"I wish we could, but Wallace doesn't trust us. Pat advised me to stay clear and let them sort it out their way, or it might blow back on us."

"Is that what you really want to do?" She knew her son well. Her instinct told her he wouldn't want to roll over for anybody.

Cole took a deep breath and let it out slow. "It's the safe play."

"Yes, but is it the right play? If they can catch these guys, it shouldn't take them long to figure out we're not involved in all of this. If not, they could be here for a long time. We've paid a steep price for what we have. I'm not going to let it fall apart on us now."

"What do you think, then?"

Nina felt backed into a corner. She had no choice.

"Get your brothers," she said. "We're going to do this our way."

THIRTY-SIX

THE SUN SET BEHIND AN OPAQUE GRAY SKY that draped the hills and valleys in growing shadows as the wolf tracked its prey through the woods. The falling snow concealed tracks and masked scents, and twice he had to double back on his own tracks to pick up the trail again. In time, it led him down one of the paths humans often took, and off it again to the other side. He stopped to shake the snow off his fur, then descended into the valley.

The wolf saw broken branches and crushed brush along one side of the valley. A long rut down the center suggested a car had come through sometime. He continued deeper into the valley and followed tire tracks around to one side.

Then he heard voices. He froze.

Slowly, he slunk low to the ground and crept along the slope until he saw a dim light just fifty feet ahead of him.

"This snow is really piling up," one of the men said. "Are these guys gonna show?"

"If they don't, we're going to have to go into town and find them. I don't have the luxury of waiting for the weather."

The wolf crept closer until he could see their dark shapes against the white snow. Even at this distance, he could smell their sweat. They leaned against two SUVs parked side by side in the middle of the valley. One of them smoked a cigarette as he leaned against the front bumper. The wolf couldn't see anything through the SUVs' blacked-out rear windows, but a fat black man sat in the driver's seat of one of them flipping through a magazine under the dome light.

"What the fuck?"

The wolf whirled when he heard the voice. The two big white guys froze when they saw him growling. One of them reached into his jacket and pulled out a pistol.

"What is that? A dog?"

"Looks like a wolf!"

The wolf heard another voice behind him ask "Hank? What's going on out there?"

The wolf backed away from them and toward the side, trying not to get caught between the two groups of men.

"C'mere, pooch . . ." The man with the gun squatted down and made beckoning gestures with his fingers. "C'mon! I'm not gonna hurt ya!"

"Jesus Christ, it's huge!" the other black man said.

The wolf barked. The man aimed a gun at him.

"Don't shoot it! Someone will hear the shot!"

"I don't want to get bit!"

"Then stay the fuck away from it!"

The wolf backed up closer to the hillside.

The man stomped in his direction and shouted. "Get away! Ya!"

In any other case, the wolf might have chewed the man's face off. The gun made him think twice. He kept backing away until he felt his tail touch brush and rock.

"That's right, beat it! Ya!"

The wolf turned and ran partway up the hill. He stopped for just a second to see if the men would chase him, and a snowball blindsided him, striking his left hip.

"Got it!"

Another snowball streaked toward the wolf. He darted forward and it struck a tree behind him. The other men picked up some snow, and suddenly it was a game for them. The wolf zigzagged its way up the hill. A snowball struck the center of his back and he kept on running until he got up out of range. The men in the valley laughed and high-fived one another.

The wolf sprinted for home. He vowed the bastards wouldn't get the drop on him next time.

THIRTY-SEVEN

"WHERE?" Wallace shouted into the radio. "Who found them?"

"They're way out on the west side of the lodge grounds," York said. "Nina says two hikers reported a pair of SUVs down in one of the valleys."

"My ass it was hikers," she told Shilling. "These people just don't listen, do they?"

"We going to check it out?" he asked.

"We don't have much choice, do we?" She keyed the mic. "Get everyone back to the lodge, now!"

Shilling drove them back to the lodge fast. The snow was piling up faster than Wallace expected, making the car slip at the turns. If Shilling could do one thing well, though, it was drive. The snow covered the trails, so he aimed the car between the trees. Wallace directed him from turn to turn on the map and used the flood light on her side to help find the edge of the trail.

Ten minutes later they arrived at the lodge and found several of their men already there. York stood near his cruiser with the Tylers gathered around him.

Wallace jumped out of the car and charged straight at them.

"Where are they?" She shoved one of their maps at Cole. "Show me on this map. Where are we going?"

"You'll never find it in this weather, Agent Wallace."

"He's right," Sheriff York said. "Nobody knows this land better than these Tyler boys."

"How convenient for you." Wallace crunched the map in her hand and threw it on the ground. "How many men do they have?"

"At least five," Cole replied.

"The hikers told you that, did they? Picked up key intel for you?"

Ronnie chuckled. Cole remained as calm as ever.

"That's what I thought."

"The point is, you need my boys to get your men out there," Nina said. "Sean and Ronnie will be happy to ride out—"

"No, Cole rides with me. Ronnie can ride with York." Wallace still didn't trust the eldest Tyler boy, or believe he was clear in this. If the Tylers were trying to pull something, she would slap the cuffs on him then and there.

"You're the boss."

Wallace rounded up the team. Counting herself, Shilling, York and his deputies, plus the two state troopers that stuck around, they had nine men. She would have liked a few more in case of surprises, but they would have to do.

"We've got at least five perps out there—probably more," she told the group. "They are almost certainly armed and dangerous. As you can see, visibility is crap. So if the shooting starts, watch your sight lines! If you get separated from the group, stay put and when this is all over, we'll find you. Any questions?"

Nobody said a word.

"Let's get out there. We'll lead."

The teams broke up and went to their cars. York took Ronnie with him, and Cole walked with Wallace to the car. As she climbed in, she spotted Nina pulling Sean to the side.

Wallace held the door open and watched them for a moment. Nina held on to Sean's arm and spoke directly into his ear. The boy nodded once, then again, and she patted him on the shoulder. He ran off around the back of the lodge building. Nina caught her watching, gave her a curt nod, and went back into the lodge through the front entrance.

"We going or what?" Shilling asked from the driver's seat.

Wallace slammed the door shut. She turned to face Cole in the back.

"When we go in, I want you and your brother to drop back. You don't need to be in the middle of this."

"What's the matter? Afraid we'll get shot and you won't be able to arrest us later?"

"Ha-ha, asshole. I haven't had any bystanders get hurt during one of my arrests and I don't plan to start tonight. It's too much paperwork."

"Mm. That would just be tragic."

They stared one another down for a moment. Cole broke it off first. He turned his head to hide a smile.

Son of a bitch, she thought. He's actually enjoying this.

THIRTY-EIGHT

DISTANT HEADLIGHTS LIT UP THE FALLING SNOW and the roar of engines filled the valley.

Rod checked his watch: 9:32. The skinheads were early, as he feared.

"Get your game faces on, boys!" Rod shouted. "Here we go!"

His crew turned on the SUV headlights. Rod stood out in front of them, flanked by Hank and Jeff. They dropped the money bags in the snow beside him. The rest of the gang fanned out, taking positions near the SUVs, but behind the headlights to help conceal their positions.

The two pickup trucks bounced and weaved through the valley. This is it, Rod thought. The home stretch. If everyone sticks to the plan, they'd be on their way home inside of fifteen minutes.

The trucks ground to a halt twenty yards from Rod. He heard the doors open, but couldn't quite make out the men coming out of them.

"What the fuck is this?" Mitch shouted. "You suddenly decide to have a convention?"

"How do you think I got your extra money up here? How do you think I'm getting the guns back?" Rod said. He couldn't help wonder why the punks on the other side of deal were always so dense.

Voices argued back and forth near the pickup. Rod couldn't make out their words, but neither of them sounded happy.

"Bring us the money and you get the guns!" Mitch said.

"Sorry, man. You come on out here and see your money. Then we load up, one vehicle at a time."

"Forget it, nigger!" someone shouted. "We set the terms!"

"Did he just say what I thought he did?" Trey shouted. All the attitude and anger of his life rising up to distort his face and make his arms go rigid—especially his trigger finger.

"Cool it," Rod said. "They're just trying to get a rise out of us."

Even as he spoke, the skinheads began to argue again.

"What's it gonna be, gentlemen? We doing this or what?"

"I'll meet you halfway," Mitch said. "Just you and the cash."

"Fine."

Rod lifted the straps, slung the two bags over his shoulders and started walking. Mitch moved toward him, blocking the headlights of his trucks. He wore combat fatigues and sported his shaved head in spite of the cold. Maybe it was the harsh light behind the figure messing with his eyesight, but Rod swore he saw smoke rising from the nazi's skull. His right hand floated near the holster on his hip. Neither of them stopped until they were near enough to shake hands.

"Here you go." Rod dropped the bags on the ground.

"Step back, boy."

Let it go, he told himself. Keep going. Rod held out his hands to show they were empty and backed off a couple of feet. Mitch dropped to one knee and unzipped the first duffel bag, the original one they came with. He riffled through the bundles of cash and found some of the broken ones.

"You trying to pull something, boy?" He waved a handful of loose bills at Rod.

"We had to spend a little to stick around. Relax, I made up for it in the other bag."

"You best not be screwing me. My men will shoot you where you stand."

“Do you want to count it here? In this shit?” Rod waved at the snow all around them. “I'm not looking to screw anyone! I just want my guns and I want to get the fuck out of here. Do we have a deal or not?”

Mitch ignored him and opened the other bag, then picked out a few bundles and fanned them. He held one out in front of the headlight beams and looked closely at the serial numbers and the presidents' faces.

Rod just wanted to get on the road and get home, and Mitch suddenly decides to get even more paranoid? He had half a mind to just give Mo and Darryl the signal and take the skinheads down.

“Alright,” the skinhead said at last. “Let's do this.”

“Pull 'em up right here and transfer the guns?”

Mitch nodded and they went to work. They had one pickup and one SUV pull up beside them. One of Trey's men opened the back door, and the skinheads dropped the tailgate.

“Pop that case,” Rod said.

Mitch gave his men the nod. One of them jumped up onto the pickup bed and released the catches on the lid of the top case, then flipped it open. Four rifles laid inside, resting in a bed of soft foam. Rod pulled out one of them, cocked the bolt and pulled the trigger. It released a satisfying click.

“Good enough.” He returned the rifle and let the men close the case.

He and Mitch stood to one side while the men transferred the cases. Rod moved into position so Mitch stood between himself and the rest of the skinheads. If they opened fire, they'd get their boss first. Mitch crossed his arms and watched his men work. It only took a few minutes to get the cases out of the pickup and into the first SUV.

So far, so good, Rod thought.

"Let's bring up the next trucks."

THIRTY-NINE

WALLACE'S STOMACH TWISTED INTO A KNOT. She had the same reaction every time she went into a raid. Shilling's driving, his wild swerves, had made it bad. Now, as they made their approach on foot, the darkness and the cold made it worse. But upchucking would have to wait. Maybe she'd get lucky and unload right on the scumbags who killed the Paulsons. Or maybe on Cole. She didn't know which would make her feel better.

Cole had said to follow the valley floor around the hill and they would run right into the perps. She hoped it wouldn't be literal. While the snowfall had slowed in the last twenty minutes, she still couldn't see more than thirty feet ahead of her.

Shilling trudged along beside her. She wished there was a way to silence the sound of their boots crushing and whooshing through the snow. The buckle on someone's shoulder strap clacked against their rifle barrel, but they had the sense to silence it.

The valley curved just as Cole said it would. Dim light shone around the bend just ahead. She held up a hand to slow everyone down. The group crept closer until she crouched down behind a tree to survey the situation. Then Shilling, York and his men all stopped behind her. They saw the halo of light and snow falling into the light from the darkness of the forest shadows.

Wallace counted four vehicles parked in a rough line out in the middle of the valley. A few men worked from the back of the pickup. The clunking of their heavy boots on the metal bed of the truck echoed across the hillside. Two more men stood out in front of the nearest SUV and seemed to be watching the transfer, while at least two more waited just past them.

Shit, she thought. Any longer and they might have missed the perps completely. She also couldn't tell exactly how many men they were dealing with. At this point, though, she didn't have much choice but to move forward.

"Spread out," she whispered to Shilling. He passed the word on to the next man, and it went on down the line. "Here we go!"

The group surged toward the vehicles, a flurry of snow and dirt flying under their charge, bodies in frenetic motion save for their arms that were steady and stiff with loaded pistols and rifles pointing at their targets below.

"Federal agents!" Wallace screamed. "Drop your weapons!"

The men around her started shouting the same. The perps scattered. Gunfire broke out. Wallace dropped to the ground and returned fire. Shotguns roared around her. She heard frantic shouting. Bullets clunked and thudded into the trucks and shattered windows and taillights.

The deputy beside her let out a grunt and fell on his face in the snow. He didn't get up.

A louder report echoed through the valley, and one of the state troopers went down screaming and clutching his shoulder. A few seconds later the snow in front of Wallace exploded and a second report sounded.

"Find cover!" she shouted. "They've got snipers in the hills!"

FORTY

COLE AND RONNIE SAW THE MUZZLE FLASHES and heard the gunshots echoing through the valley. They had followed the team down the trail, but hung back a hundred feet to observe. They heard Wallace's shout about the sniper, and Cole could just make out the deputies scrambling for cover behind the trees.

"They're getting eaten alive," Cole said.

A growl sounded behind them. They turned to see a figure covered in dark fur approaching them. It had the head of a wolf, but walked on two legs like a man. It bared its teeth in a wicked snarl. Sharp claws curled out from its fingertips.

"Hold up, Sean," Ronnie told the creature.

Cole didn't say anything. He watched the muzzle flashes popping off in time with the gunshots.

"We let 'em die, they're off our back. There's no doubt about who killed the Paulsons anymore. They may send more feds, but they won't be on our trail."

"Pat and his men are out there, too."

"You tell me, then, bro. What's our play?"

Cole held up his right hand. His fingers curled as the muscles contracted and claws curved out from his finger tips. Black fur pushed out through the skin along the back of his hand and out from under his sleeve.

"You and me, we need to talk about this moral compass of yours." Ronnie took off his jacket. "Sean, get up there and find those snipers. We'll be right behind you."

Sean threw back his head and howled, then sprinted up the hill.

FORTY-ONE

ROD AIMED FOR THE FEDS' MUZZLE FLASHES and squeezed off a few shots.

"Get in the trucks!" Mitch shouted at his men. "We're leaving right now!"

On the other side of Rod, Dane aimed his rifle across the hood of the pickup. He emptied an entire magazine, swapped in a fresh one, and started shooting again. He laughed all the while. One of Trey's men jumped behind the wheel of a SUV, trying to maneuver around the first pickup. Then the rear tire blew out and the SUV lurched to that side. The wheel spun in the snow and kicked up mud, but the SUV hardly moved.

Rod crouched down in front of the second SUV to reload. Bullets slammed into its side to his left. The windshield exploded above him. He could see Hank further out. The big guy ducked behind a tree as he reloaded his revolver. He didn't see any sign of Jeff, so he sidestepped and peered around the other side of the vehicle.

Trey jumped out of the crippled SUV and moved to the rear quarter panel to return fire. One of his crew was splayed out in the snow a few feet past him, bleeding from the side of his face near where an eye had been. The crack of a rifle sounded around them every few seconds as the snipers earned their pay.

It's all going to hell, Rod thought. Even if he got away, how much did the feds know? If they had identified him, or even Hank or Jeff, they wouldn't get far. They could drive out of the valley and right into a roadblock. Best case, there would be an APB and every law enforcement agency in the state would be on the lookout for him. Running deep into the mountains, then heading north for the border sounded better and better.

The headlight assembly exploded beside him, and he shielded his face with his pistol hand.

First things first: he leaned over and squeezed off two shots at one of the muzzle flashes.

A howl echoed through the valley.

"What the fuck was that?"

FORTY-TWO

COLE CAST OFF HIS CLOTHING as dark fur sprouted across his body. His joints cracked and popped as bones reconfigured around them. Hidden muscles throughout his chest and limbs tensed and shifted into place. His nose and mouth came together and pushed forward, stretching into a wolf's snout. Fangs and incisors protruded from his distended jaw. His ears pulled back along his flattening skull and cupped forward to points at the ends. His knees buckled and his hips shifted. Adrenaline surged through his veins, filling him with an insatiable hunger and rage that could not be quelled.

Neither man nor animal, yet somehow both, this form knew nothing of flight—only fight. It separated Cole from his senses, leaving a primal beast he both feared and reviled. It felt to him like a monster pulling at the end of a frayed leash on which he had only a tenuous grasp. It existed only to kill, and more often than not, its release resulted in death.

Beside him, pain wracked Ronnie's body as he endured the same changes, and he reveled in it. He embraced the strength and the power of the beast, and found exhilaration in the pursuit of his prey. It defined him, set him apart from the men and the animals. The beast should be feared and reviled, not locked in a cage of weaker flesh. He flexed his claws and longed for the feel of hot rushing blood and cracking bones beneath them.

The brothers rose up on their new feet and howled into the wind. Their differences did not matter. Tonight, they would hunt together.

Tonight, they would kill together.

FORTY-THREE

MO PUT THE CROSSHAIRS OVER THE COP'S NECK and pulled the trigger. His rifle boomed and bucked, and a red mist exploded across the sight picture as the cop went down.

He grinned as he shifted his rifle to find his next target. This made the long wait in the snow worthwhile. The wet clothing, the numb chest, the frozen balls—they all went away the moment he pumped the first bullet into the valley. His trigger finger itched when the skinheads showed up, but nothing beat the thrill of taking down a bunch of pigs. He'd have done this shit for free.

The scope swept over a figure hiding behind a tree. Mo almost missed him in the darkness, but his pale face peeked out around the narrow tree trunk. He wore a knit cap and a dark jacket. After a few seconds, he leaned around the tree and fired a few shots toward the trucks.

The guy moved too much for Mo to get a clean shot. He would have to flush him out. He put the crosshairs near the edge of the tree and fired. The bark shattered and the fed disappeared back around the other side. Mo shifted his aim to the other side of the tree, fired gain. The guy rabbited.

Mo tracked him through the snow. Branches and trunks rolled through the sight picture.

"C'mon, you son of a bitch . . ."

Just then the sight cleared up. The fed was a dark blob in the falling snow, with FBI written clearly across his back. Mo squeezed the trigger.

BLAM!

The fed did a nosedive into the snow and didn't move again.

"Next!"

He tracked through the darkness. A muzzle flash caught his attention. He found the pistol and followed the arm up to the shooter and found a woman's head. She looked over toward the fallen fed, giving him a better look at her face.

"Hey there, baby." It would almost be a shame to put a bullet through such a hottie.

Almost. His finger tightened around the trigger.

A growl sounded to his left. Mo looked up to see a snarling, hairy beast running straight at him. His breath hitched in his throat as he rolled to one side and pointed his rifle at the creature. It ducked and rolled and his first shot went high. It got back to its feet and leapt at him and his next shot went wide.

Then its claws were in his chest, and this time he did scream. He screamed so loud his voice cracked and broke, and he could feel the creature's hot breath on his face as the piercing pain in his ribs went deeper and deeper.

Mo felt his rifle across his belly, trapped between himself and the creature. He pushed with all his might and the wolfish jaws snapped at his eyes and nose. Spittle sprayed his face.

“Help!” Mo shouted.

The creature pulled its right hand back. Its claws raked the insides of Mo's ribs, pulling out strips of his flesh where the claws dug into his side. He almost blacked out. Then its fist slammed into his face and his arms went limp. The creature collapsed against him. Its jaws opened wide and Mo gasped for another breath.

The creature's teeth clamped down around his neck. Mo choked on his own blood as he tried again to push the creature away, but the strength drained from his limbs. Shock spared him the white-hot pain of his throat being torn out, but he felt the tugging and tearing and heard the wet gurgle of his dying breath.

The rifle slipped from his still fingers.

FORTY-FOUR

WALLACE SPOTTED A SHADOW MOVING AWAY from the nearer SUV. She took careful aim and squeezed off two shots. The slide on her pistol locked back on an empty magazine, but the shadow dropped. She ducked back around the tree and swapped in a new magazine, then turned back and drew a bead on the machine gun muzzle flash. It stopped for a moment when she fired on it, then resumed a moment later from a new position.

"Shit!"

"You alright, partner?" she called.

"I'm going to try to flank those snipers! Cover me!"

Wallace and the other officers opened up. Glass shattered. Head and taillights exploded and winked out on the vehicles. The perps' guns fell silent for a moment as they ducked for cover. Shilling sprinted across the snow, circling around Wallace and the other officers. He reappeared in her peripheral vision to her left as he ran for the hill.

Then he fell.

"Brian?"

He didn't move. Wallace looked around and counted two officers down: one not moving and the other screaming and pressing his hands to a wound in his leg. York spoke into the radio mic on his shoulder. Every time he stopped to listen to a response, he pressed shotgun shells into the magazine.

The perps started shooting again. Wallace took cover behind a tree. One of the pickup engines roared behind her.

She hated letting any of them escape, but at the same time, it would cut the perps' numbers down. It shouldn't be too difficult to track down a bullet-riddled pickup and match it to an owner. The second pickup wouldn't get far in this weather with its headlights shot out.

Her gun ran empty again, leaving her with just two more magazines on her belt. She tried not to think about Shilling as she reloaded, about his wife and his three-year-old son.

Just live through this, she told herself.

FORTY-FIVE

HANK CROUCHED DOWN BESIDE JEFF.

"How you doing?"

"Conserving ammo until I can see something," Jeff said. "You?"

"Same. How many do you think there are?"

"I can't tell. I'd say no more than a dozen, judging by the flashes. Less now."

"Whattaya say we flank 'em?"

"Lead the way."

The two cowboys crouched low and hustled to the hillside, following it along the valley toward the cops. They stopped and took cover. No fire came their way.

"You ready?" Hank whispered.

"Let's rock."

They rolled out of cover and strode toward the cops, side by side, pistols raised. Jeff shot the first officer through the head. Hank shot the next just under his left arm. The third spotted them and took a shot at them. Hank and Jeff scattered and returned fire. The deputy shouted but kept shooting at Hank. Jeff aimed and snapped off a shot. The deputy's head rocked back and he went down.

Another cop came up on one knee with his shotgun to his shoulder. He fired, pumped, fired again. The blasts knocked Hank flat on his back.

Jeff fired on the cop. The bullet sparked off the side of the shotgun and the cop yelped and dropped the weapon. Another officer took a shot at him. He dropped to one knee and shot back. The officer screamed and fell back on her ass. The revolver's hammer clicked home on spent chambers.

Jeff had never shot a bitch before, but there was a first time for everything. He knelt down beside Hank and picked up his pistol to finish the job.

FORTY-SIX

DARRYL PICKED UP HIS RIFLE and moved down the ridge in search of a better shot. He managed a few shots early. But then, the trees and darkness conspired against him. He took a second position, aimed through the scope. He didn't see a damn thing as he scanned the valley.

"Come on, come on . . ."

He took a deep breath of the frigid air. No way he could let any of these cops out of here. If they caught him they'd put him away for life, if not give him the chair for this shootout. He lifted his head and spotted the muzzle flashes, then shifted the barrel and sighted them in.

Still no clear shot.

Darryl sighed and picked up his rifle again. He craned his neck over the hillside as he ran, trying to get a better bead on the muzzle flashes. Then he smacked into something and fell flat on his back.

His hand scrambled for the dropped rifle as he tried to see what he hit. It didn't feel like a tree.

A wolf stared down at him. It reached down and grabbed the rifle, its claws clicking across the stock. Darryl just stared at it, mouth agape, as his brain tried to correlate the almost human hand with the snarling animal. It ripped the rifle out of his hands and raised it back over its shoulder like a baseball bat.

The rifle butt slammed into the side of his head the instant it occurred to him to scream.

FORTY-SEVEN

MITCH JUMPED OVER FENTON'S BODY and climbed into the passenger side of the pickup.

"Go! Go! Go!"

Gage scrambled over the side and into the truck bed.

"What about Dane?" Duff asked.

"He's on his own!"

Duff mashed the gas and wrestled the wheel around. The rear tires spun and then caught, and the bed swerved around. Gage smacked into the side wall, then sat up and leaned against the wheel well as Duff righted the pickup. Gage popped off a few shots into the black hill.

"The feds catch those niggers, they're gonna talk," Duff said.

"We can't worry about that right now."

"You got the money?"

"It's in the truck." Mitch looked back and verified the bags were still back there. They slid around with Gage, but they were still there.

"That's all that matters."

A heavy thud sounded behind them and the truck bounced on its suspension.

"What was that?"

Mitch turned in time to see Gage slam into the back window. It shattered and the pieces clattered to the floor and across the seat. Mitch shielded his eyes for a moment, and when he looked again he saw Gage flung out over the tailgate and off the truck. He thought the arm coming through the window belonged to a man in a fur coat until he grabbed the wrist and felt the thick, coarse bristles and the tight muscles underneath.

An elbow struck him between the eyes and he let go. Duff hollered and pushed away from the wheel as the claw-tipped hands found his throat and raked across it. Blood sprayed the steering wheel and the inside of the windshield. Then the arm was gone and the truck veered toward a tree.

Mitch threw up his hands a split second before the front end wrapped itself around the tree trunk. The airbag exploded and Mitch disappeared into it. His right shin struck the underside of the console. Then he bounced back into the seat. He blinked and tried to get his bearings. The airbags hung deflated from the dash and steering column.

Duff lay across the wheel. Blood dripped out of the ragged slash in his throat and drenched the pale airbag fabric.

Mitch's bowels clenched when he heard the snarling next to him. A wolf peered in at him, and it tried to open the door, but the mangled fender and side ruined the hinges and blocked the door. Mitch scrambled across Duff's back and grabbed the driver's side door handle. The door opened a few inches and he ignored the pain in his leg as he got to his knees and shoved Duff through the gap. Duff's body fell out and hit the ground with a crack that sounded like his neck snapping.

A hand wrapped around Mitch's ankle. He turned over and kicked at it, striking only the doorframe and window ledge at first. Then the wolf-thing hauled him through the shattered window, shredding the exposed skin of his face, forcing a scream he did not expect. He landed hard in the snow. His head clipped the running board on the way down. He saw stars and he grabbed the back of his head.

The wolf's claws swiped across Mitch's face. He could feel the tips scraping bone. The coarse grinding rattled through his skull. His right eye popped, and warmth gushed across his face and down his neck. He screamed and brought his hands to his face in a vain attempt to hold in place the shredded remains of his cheeks and nose.

The next rake went across his chest in one direction, then another in the opposite direction. He screamed and tried to cover his chest this time. Then, the claws found his belly. Every time he shifted his hands, the claws found him again, tearing at his body, at his arms, at his face over and over. He sputtered and plead through the blood until at last the assault stopped. Blood covered his remaining good eye, blurring his vision. He heard the heavy breathing.

Those cruel hands wrapped up fistfuls of Mitch's fatigues near his shoulders and hoisted him to his feet. Mitch dangled, limp, as the wolf slammed him against the side of the truck.

"Please," he moaned.

The wolf ripped his belly again. He clutched at the wound and felt slick loops of flesh slip through his fingers. A wet splash hit the snow, and the wolf dropped him. He saw it run back into the snow as his vision faded.

FORTY-EIGHT

THE SLIGHTEST MOVEMENT SENT WAVES of burning pain radiating from Wallace's hip. She couldn't move her leg, and just the effort of sitting up hurt so bad she almost vomited. Sweat broke out across her face and warm shivers fired through her chest and stomach. She still had her gun in her hand, though, and she refused to count herself out yet.

Sheriff York knelt on one knee at her side. He raised his pistol and took aim at something out past her feet. If only she could see!

A gunshot. Another. York rocked back. His pistol fired harmlessly into the air and he collapsed near her head.

"No!" She grabbed her pistol with her left hand and fought the pain as she pushed herself up onto her right elbow.

Jeff kicked the gun out of her hand. She looked up past his pistol into his face as he thumbed back the hammer on his revolver.

"Too bad I couldn't fuck you before I killed you." He winked at her.

Someone big tackled him. Both men tumbled out of her vision beyond the tree beside her. One of the other officers?

She could hear the sounds of their struggle, their limbs thrashing through the snow and fallen leaves and the grunts and strains of their effort. One of them let out a low and guttural growl.

I need to find my gun, she thought. She grabbed the tree and tried to pull herself up, only to scream and collapse to her back again.

A wave of dizziness overcame her, and she blacked out.

FORTY-NINE

JEFF FELT LIKE A TRUCK HIT HIM. His shoulder crunched into the ground and he and his assailant rolled across the snow. He lost one of the guns, but he pressed the other into the guy's gut and pulled the trigger. It snapped on spent cartridges.

A swiping claw knocked the gun out of his hand, and only then did he realize this was no man.

The wolf punched him high on the right cheekbone. The impact spun his head around and he landed face-first, his blood spraying out in the snow in front of him. It picked him up by the back of his jacket and bit his shoulder. The teeth dug into his deltoid and crushed his clavicle. He felt the bone snap under the pressure.

Jeff sucked up the pain and threw his left elbow into the creature's gut. It's grip loosened enough for him to wriggle out of it. He fell and rolled onto his back. Did it have balls? He threw a high kick into the monster's groin.

It let out a yelp, but recovered and pounced on him almost immediately. Jeff threw up his left arm and the monster latched on to his forearm like a bulldog. It chewed and jerked its head back and forth. Jeff tried to get his legs under its hips to shove it away. His right arm wouldn't do what he told it to do.

Jeff shouted at last, more in frustration than pain, and finally got his heels into the wolf's hips. He rolled the wolf onto its side and pulled his left arm loose. Most of his sleeve and a fair chunk of meat tore away. He got up and ran for the SUVs, leaving a trail of blood and echoing screams.

The monster tackled him again. It shoved his face into the snow and this time he screamed for help. The snow and mud stifled his cries. The monster yanked the back of his collar down, then bit him on the back of his neck. It let go, but still pinned his face to the ground. He could feel the points of its claws digging into his scalp and just below his ear.

He felt its other hand reach down around his neck. With one quick swipe, it tore out the front and side of his throat. His legs kicked and shuddered as he coughed blood through the hole.

FIFTY

ROD AND TREY STOOD SIDE-BY-SIDE near the SUV, still aiming their guns toward the feds' position.

"I can't see a damn thing," Trey said.

Rod concentrated. He thought he heard someone moving around out in the field of black in front of them, then nothing. A radio crackled to life. A woman's voice came through. Rod couldn't make out the words. It went silent for several seconds, then came back. Nobody responded to her.

"Maybe they pulled back."

"Or we killed 'em all!" Dane sounded proud, triumphant. He walked past them and turned Fenton over with his boot. "Poor bastard."

One of Trey's guys came around the SUV.

"Anyone else left, Jim?" Trey asked.

The guy shook his head.

"Let's get the hell out of here," Rod said. "Hank? Jeff?"

No answer. He called out to them again.

"Shit. Call the snipers down."

"Hey Mo! Darryl! Come on down!"

Rod shoved his pistol into his waistband and checked the SUV's tire. It wasn't going anywhere. They'd have to move all the guns to the good SUV and hope they fit.

Trey called for his guys again. Dane lifted Fenton into the bed of the pickup.

Someone rustled through the trees up on the hillside.

"Mo? Is that you?"

Something hit the ground behind them. Footsteps crunched through the snow.

Dane fired a burst of his machine gun into the darkness. The footsteps stopped.

Rod's palm sweated around his pistol grip. A fed? The SUVs headlights were pointed in the wrong direction. He wondered if they could just drive on out of there and leave the fed or whomever it was behind.

Another rustle behind them, then Jim hollered in pain and fright. Rod whirled around, holding up his gun, but Jim was already gone. He heard a muffed gasping sound in the darkness beyond the SUV. Trey circled to the left.

"Jim!" he shouted. "Jim, you okay?"

"Fuck this!" Dane fired bursts of his machine gun to the front and to the back.

"Stop, my guy's out there!"

Dane ignored him, and Rod didn't argue. Dane's gun ran dry. He popped the magazine and let it fall to the ground.

A howl erupted behind Rod. He threw up his arms to protect his head and hunched his shoulders as someone hit Trey and took him down to the ground.

"What the fuck is that?" Dane yelled.

Rod turned and saw an animal had pounced on Trey. He lifted his pistol to shoot, but the thing looked him in the eye and he froze. He saw intelligence in its gleaming eyes, almost a smile in the snarl. Before he could pull the trigger, the thing hoisted Trey in front of its chest. Rod fired and put two bullets into his friend. Trey went limp in the thing's grip.

Dane got his magazine in and rocked the rifle's bolt back. The animal leapt off of Trey. Rod tried to shoot it again and missed. Dane opened up with his assault rifle, firing from the hip. The animal disappeared.

"Did you see that fuckin' thing? Was that a wolf?"

The pistol trembled in Rod's grip. He had no idea where it was. He kept the pistol raised in the direction where it disappeared while backing up toward the SUV. Screw the guns, he needed to get the fuck out of there.

The animal thudded on top of the SUV's roof and growled at them. Both men raised their guns, and the animal jumped off the back side. Their bullets punched through the empty air.

Then Rod saw another animal leap out of the darkness toward Dane. The beast raked at his back with its claws. He screamed and kicked and tried to get the thing off of him.

Rod ran. He turned his back on the vehicles and sprinted with all his might toward the other end of the valley. With luck he could lose the creatures in the darkness and flag down a passing car on the highway. The cold air seared his lungs, but he kept on running.

Then he heard rustling behind him. He dared not look back, but the sound drew closer and louder. Rod poured it on, pumping his legs and arms as fast as he could. It had to be the animal behind him, and still he sensed it was almost upon him. He said a silent prayer, extended the pistol back behind him and started shooting.

His shots went well wide of the wolf-thing pursuing him, and even now it moved to the left to stay clear of his line of fire. The pistol's slide locked back.

"No!"

The wolf tackled him to the ground. Its claws ripped through his jacket and his flesh with equal ease. He rolled to his side and tried to defend himself, but the beast just chewed up his arm and ripped at his chest and neck. He screamed with all his might until all energy left him entirely. The wolf pinned Rod's mangled arm to the ground and exposed his neck.

Teeth punched through his flesh and punctured his throat. A gush of hot arterial blood splattered the underside of his jaw. The wolf shook its head and he felt a sickening crunch at the back of his neck. Rod died listening to his last breath burbling through his torn larynx.

FIFTY-ONE

THE BOUNCING WOKE WALLACE.

The pain followed, but she could not shake the groggy feeling that overcame her. She was upside down. No, she realized, she was draped over someone's shoulder. Cold air rushed by. She could just make out the blur of trees and snow.

"Who's that?"

Her Samaritan did not answer. It had to be the same guy who saved her from the redneck. Who was left? Where were York and his men? Where was—

Oh no, Brian.

The Samaritan jumped over a fallen tree limb. The impact on the other side jarred her hip and the pain almost knocked her senseless. She recognized the onset of shock.

She needed medical help or she would bleed out all over this guy's back.

Her face bumped up against his jacket. It felt soft and warm, not like her Gore-Tex. She pulled up her hand to feel it and bumped something rigid just below her head. It bobbed as the Samaritan ran. She wrapped her fingers around it. The same soft stuff ran down its length. If she didn't know better, she'd swear it was a fur-covered tail.

Another leap across a narrow creak sent a fresh jolt of pain through her body.

Wallace passed out again.

FIFTY-TWO

"PUT HER OVER HERE."

The voice sounded muffled, as if it rose from the depths of a vast sea. Light burned red through her eyelids. She opened them and let the light stab at her eyes. A dark shape leaned over her head. A hand, warm and soothing, pressed against her cheek. It went away after a second and unzipped her jacket.

Her eyes started to adjust. A dark-skinned woman opened her pants.

"Tyler?" Wallace croaked.

"Hush. You need your strength."

"What're . . . you doing?" Wallace craned her neck for a better look. Nina took a heavy pair of shears to her jeans. Blood covered her hands.

"Trying to save your life."

The room spun. Wallace dropped her head to the pillow and let it roll to one side. She could just make out a tall figure standing in the shadows in the corner of the room.

"I didn't know you had a dog," Wallace mumbled.

"I said hush!"

Wallace closed her eyes. She felt very cold and tired. The pain in her hip grew more and more distant until she let it slip away completely.

EPILOGUE

WALLACE FLIPPED THROUGH THE PICTURES over and over.

The Bureau sent in more men, and they identified her bad guys: Rod Babineaux, Jeff McLean and Henry Owens. They also uncovered the rest of the story: the three of them attempted to purchase a cache of firearms from a local skinhead group. The bullets from the Paulson murders matched one of the skinheads' rifles, and the fingerprints on the rifle belonged to Donald "Dane" Ramsey, a man with a jacket heavy with violent crime and prison time.

In fact, the investigators explained everything except how Babineaux, Ramsey and most of the other perps died. They hoped Wallace, as the lone survivor, could offer some clue, but she couldn't remember anything that might have caused the wounds in the pictures. None of the officers left the firing line, and the positions of their bodies supported that.

She stared at the picture of Babineaux's mauled body. Maybe a point blank shotgun blast could have done that kind of damage, or a machete or an axe. But the scene photos and diagrams demonstrated none of her men got that close. The autopsy said a hunting knife with a gut hook could have done it, but to Wallace, the ragged wounds resembled those of some animal attacks, such as those of a cougar or lynx. The autopsy also found punctures consistent with bites on some of the victims, but those more closely resembled the bites of a large dog or wolf.

The medical examiner concluded that the wounds were the result of an animal attack, but the Bureau agents on the scene were skeptical. Even Wallace hesitated to sign off on it. The Tylers' report claimed they stayed well back from the gunfight, and Wallace confirmed they had not been armed with knives or guns when they guided the officers out to the valley.

Wallace slapped the manila folder shut in disgust and tossed the whole thing on the gimbaled table beside her bed. She hesitated to turn on the television due to the near-constant coverage of the shootout. Her boss and the higher-ups stuck with a no-comment policy, and the hospital staff—including security—had to stay on their toes to keep members of the media out of her room. The newspaper in the trash beside her bed ran the picture from her Bureau ID and called her a hero for surviving the shootout.

Courage? More like luck. The media could call her a hero all they wanted; she knew it would only be a matter of time before her boss lost patience with her lack of answers.

Someone knocked on her door.

"Come in."

Cole Tyler poked his head in.

"I can't say I expected to see you, Mr. Tyler. What can I do for you?"

"How are you doing?"

"I'll be a lot better when they let me walk again." She pointed to the thick mass of bandages surrounding her hip.

"How bad is it?"

"The bullet cracked my pelvis and dislocated my hip. I'll be in here another couple of days, and then I'm looking at a lot of physical therapy. I suppose it could be worse, though. If you hadn't pulled me out of there, I would have died."

"How well do you remember that?"

"Not very." She shrugged. "I was pretty out of it, but I feel like you carried me back. Is that right?"

"Only to the cars. It's a long way to carry someone back to the cabins."

"This is going to sound strange, but . . . do you have a fur coat?"

"No, why?"

"It's not important. I should thank your mom, too. They tell me she did a good job keeping me from bleeding to death and treating my shock."

"It's basic first aid," Cole said. "It can be a long wait at the lodge if one of our hunters gets injured. We try to be ready for anything."

"Just the same, thanks. To both of you."

"You're welcome."

"Level with me for a moment, would you?"

"Sure."

"What really happened out there?"

"I don't know what you mean."

"Oh, come off it, Cole!" She picked up the manila folder and pull out two pictures of Rod Babineaux's ravaged body. She flipped them to the foot of the bed. "Look at those! Tell me you don't know how that happened!"

Cole didn't touch the photos. "Like we told the other agents, we have no idea. Ronnie says he heard a howl after the shooting started. Maybe they stumbled onto a den of wolves."

"Do you really believe that?"

"Agent Wallace, I've got people telling the media a family of Bigfoots jumped in and tore these guys apart.

What makes more sense, mountain legends or a pack of terrified animals?"

"Animals don't pick and choose their victims. They can't tell the difference between the good guys and the bad guys, which is exactly what happened that night."

Cole chuckled.

"What's funny?"

"I didn't expect an interrogation, that's all." He fiddled with some of the flowers arranged on the table along the wall opposite Wallace's bed. "By the way, sorry I didn't bring flowers. I figured a donation would be more appropriate."

"A donation to whom?"

"The International Wolf Center up in Ely." Cole pulled a card out of his pocket and handed it over.

Sure enough, the card featured a logo of running wolves. The Tylers had donated fifty dollars in her name.

"You're kidding, right?"

"Absolutely not," Cole said. "It's one of our favorite charities."

Wallace put the card on the table. She really hated that she couldn't read him. Was this sarcasm? Did he honestly believe a pack of wolves had come to her rescue? Or was he making fun of the medical examiner's assessment and the Bureau's lack of a better explanation? She reigned in her irritation.

"Thanks," she said.

"I best get going. Pat's funeral is in a couple of hours."

"Pass my condolences along to his family, would you?"

"Of course. Take care of yourself, Agent Wallace."

"See you soon."

Cole shot her an uncertain look, then he nodded and left.

Wallace lowered the top of the bed with the wired control box resting beside her. As she lay flat, she turned to look at the photos lying by her feet. She hated secrets. If the Tylers didn't kill Babineaux and the skinheads, they knew a lot more than they let on. It sounded a lot like Nevada, giving the Tylers two big secrets.

She vowed the Tylers would keep neither for long.

AFTERWORD

This all started with a murder.

I walked out of a store on some crummy errand or another and I saw it plain as day. A young man falls down in the desert. A boot appears on the back of his neck, and the camera floats up a uniformed leg to a .45. Higher still and we see a grizzled sheriff staring down at the young man.

Bang.

A young woman runs past him, screaming. A deputy chases her. The sheriff raises his pistol.

Bang.

The camera follows the path of the bullet. It streaks past the deputy's ear toward the woman. It slams into the back of her head. The screen goes dark, then the bullet and the camera reach daylight on the other side.

I sat in the car for a few minutes to write it all down in my notebook. It had been so vivid I could see the characters' features, the sheriff's boots, badge and uniform, the girl's red, flower-print sundress flowing in the breeze. I didn't care where it came from, what I wanted to figure out was what to do with it.

A screenplay seemed obvious at the time. I imagined the credits playing across the desert scene, with a rockin' Southern-rock soundtrack. The music stops. The wind blows. Then *BAM!*, action.

Only problem is, I'd never written a screenplay before, and had only read a few, so I didn't really know the format. Second, I had no contacts at the time to get this thing in front of people who mattered in the industry. Finally, there was zero guarantee this scene would show up in a form anywhere close to what I pictured by the time studio notes, the director, and the effects crew got their hands on it.

Three strikes, you're out.

I never give up on an idea, though, and when I learned the owners of my new comic shop also ran Moonstone Books, I asked if I could pitch them something. They said yes, and I had nothing. So I went home and remembered that scene. Its visual intensity would carry over to the comic page, and there was a good chance the artist would keep it as is.

Excellent. I sat down at the keyboard to write and promptly realized I had no idea why the sheriff killed these kids. Was he an anti-hero or a villain? What did they do to deserve this? Even better, what happened next?

I had just finished an abortive attempt at a crime novel, so I had crime on the brain. I thought maybe the kid was a drug dealer and the antihero cop took him down. Or maybe the kids saw something they shouldn't have. I kicked around a few more possibilities, but none of them really grabbed me or answered the question, "what next?"

So why not make it a supernatural thriller? Make the kid a monster of some kind, and now the sheriff has a reason to blow him away. Make him a werewolf, and now the sheriff has silver bullets. That's when the "what next?" clicked into place: the rest of his pack comes looking for him. That turned into his brother, and from there the first comic book miniseries, *Werewolves: Call of the Wild*, came to be.

We didn't get a full series off the ground, but it still didn't want to die. When Nina (then only known as "Mom") made a cameo in the first issue of W:CotW, I had a pretty good idea of the family's back story. Each of the family members had their own story to tell, and they fit together in a nice arc.

About that time, A.N. Ommus at Evileye Books started flirting with me. I initially discussed a different book with him, but as he shared his formula for world domination, it became clear that book just wasn't big enough. Evileye wanted a series, and I wanted in on his plans, so I pitched him *The Pack*.

Which brings us to the book you just read.

Winter Kill is a new beginning for the Tyler family, the first book in a series made up of prose fiction and graphic novels. Each book will feature a stand-alone story, but the events of each volume will be inter-connected. I have big plans for the characters and the series, and I hope you'll continue to follow along as I keep asking the characters, "what next?"

Thanks for reading, and welcome to *The Pack*.

Mike Oliveri
October 2009
Peoria

EXCLUSIVE EXCERPT

LIE WITH THE DEAD

Book Two in *The Pack*

Werewolf Noir Series

By Mike Oliveri

ONE

A GLIMMER IN THE DUSTY ROAD AHEAD caught Angie's eye, but by the time she recognized the spike strip, it was too late. Her front tires hissed and popped. Angie seized the wheel with both hands as the rear tires blew. Her foot hovered over the brake as the steering went spongy. The rented Malibu shuddered and lurched on its rims, spraying gravel into the wheel wells and kicking clouds of dust up in a whirlwind trail. Someone wanted her stopped. All the better in the middle of desert wasteland where bodies are nothing more than fertilizer.

She goosed the gas instead. The left front tire unraveled and flogged the quarter panel. The car slid off the main strip onto the pothole-pocked shoulder. The fender missed the corner of the faded and rotted "Welcome to Charity" sign by inches. The wheel rammed against the edges of the potholes. The impacts threw Angie forward and the seatbelt caught her hip, setting off an explosion of pain rivaling the bullet that shattered her hip in the snowy fields of the Tyler Lodge grounds six months back. She bit back screams as every little bump in the crumbling asphalt jolted her back and ass. She fought the urge to slam on the brakes as she steered back onto the desert road and barreled down Main Street and into the abandoned town.

A thunderclap erupted off her left shoulder. The rear passenger window exploded. Tiny chunks of glass sprayed across the back seat. Something bit her just below the right ear. Two more shots came in rapid succession, and the rear window shattered and fell.

Angie kept her head down. The shooter had to be in one of the boarded-up storefronts she just passed. She swerved left as she approached the next intersection, then spun the wheel around to the right. The Malibu leaned into the turn, and the front left rim collapsed. The chassis bounced hard and ground across the asphalt. She jammed on the brakes, then threw off her seatbelt as the car shuddered to a halt. Her hand went straight to the .40-caliber SIG behind her hip as she pushed through the door and out of the car. Ducking low, she moved around the door and crouched behind the engine block. She extended the pistol over the hood in a two-handed grip and scanned the right side of the street.

She expected Old West. Instead, Main Street Charity looked more Mayberry meets Omega Man. It looked like a quaint old place where kids would frequent soda shops and greasers would race muscle cars up and down the strip, until one day they all just up and left, abandoning it all to the desert winds.

A man stepped out of a doorway three doors down, one hand shielding his eyes from the sun, the other holding a long, black shotgun.

Angie sighted the man's center of mass. "Federal Agent! Drop the gun!"

The man froze. Angie recognized the panicked look, the tension of his body as he raised the weapon. She fired three quick shots and dropped him.

A bullet zipped past her head and the whipcrack of a rifle shot echoed down the street. She ducked down beside the wheel. The tang of melted rubber stung her nostrils. A second shot, then a third thudded into the hood.

"Ahh, shit . . ." The first shooter's shotgun rattled and clacked against the street. Angie looked beneath the car to spot him, but the lowered chassis due to the flattened tires made it difficult to see more than a few feet beyond the passenger side.

"You alright?" someone shouted. Another male, this one with a deep, booming voice. Probably the sniper.

"I'm fine!" the first shooter responded. "She hit my vest."

"How about you, lady? You drop your gun, poke that pretty little head out, maybe I won't blow it off!"

Pretty little head indeed. It went one of two ways with the bad guys: they either see the dark red hair and green eyes and think they can charm her out of her pants, or they see a slender woman just shy of five seven and think they can take her down easy. She enjoyed proving them wrong.

"Come on now," Sniper shouted. "Let's do this the easy way so no one gets hurt!"

His voice echoed down the street, making it difficult to pinpoint Shotgun's footsteps. He crossed to her side of the street, but she couldn't be sure how far away. Her bullets would slow him down some, even with the vest, but if he got close enough with that shotgun, he didn't need to be at the top of his game.

Angie crawled to the front of the car and peeked around the front bumper. Shotgun slipped into a recessed doorway two doors down. The whipcrack of the rifle echoed down the street again, and the bullet whacked the sidewalk two feet from the car's nose. Angie ducked back again, and a second bullet struck the sidewalk just a few yards ahead of the first. He had to be on the left side of the street, probably on the second floor.

"Last chance, lady!" Sniper shouted. "Next one doesn't miss!"

Hurried footsteps came closer, then shuffled aside. Shotgun was moving in. She couldn't stay here. Sniper would just keep her pinned down until Shotgun had a clear shot. The jewelry store in front of her had a recessed doorway, and the glass had been broken out of the door, but it was directly across from the passenger side and she didn't like the idea of having to run toward her shooters to get there. Running farther down the street guaranteed a bullet in the back, so she eyeballed the corner of the jewelry store.

If there were more gunmen coming to flank her from around that corner, it would be real trouble.

She didn't see any other option. She got off her knees and onto her toes, settling into a sprinter's starting position. Her hip burned from the tension. Footsteps approached, then another shuffle as Shotgun moved into the jewelry store's doorway.

Angie lunged forward, leading with her pistol. Shotgun started to bring up his weapon, then ducked back as she pulled the trigger. Her shot went wide, but it had the desired effect of backing him off. She sprinted around the corner and kept running across the street toward the back of the next building. The rifle barked behind her, but she was well out of sight now.

She leapt onto the next curb, stopped and spun. She swept her pistol across the narrow road behind the buildings and, seeing no signs of movement, shifted her aim to the corner of the jewelry store.

Shotgun peeked around the corner.

She put two rounds into the brick beside him. He ducked back for cover and she ran around behind the next building.

The street came off at a diagonal from the main street, passing a triangular lot with a rickety jungle gym and a crooked merry-go-round behind the jewelry store. The street continued past the abandoned gas station across from her. An alley stretched out in front of her for another block, with the backs of the Main Street stores on her left and the back yards of some homes on her right. A battered chain-link fence surrounded the gravel lot behind the service station, enclosing only the decaying hulks of three ancient cars and a stripped pickup.

She knew she had to get out of the alley quick. Sniper might be about to pop out a back door, or he might be regrouping with Shotgun so they could track her together. If they were smart—and she had to assume they were to set up an ambush—they'd have one man down Main Street and one covering the alley. They'd have the luxury of flushing her out one way or the other, or just sitting tight and waiting for backup. If she followed her first instinct and went into one of the buildings, it put her in their waiting game.

She sprinted across the alley and past the service station's lot, then ducked alongside the fence as she ran toward the back of the building. Her hip tightened up and burned, but she endured and darted across the yard between the service station and the first house. Her hiking boots crunched in the gravel drive, then she was up on the porch with her back to the wall.

Breathe, she told herself. She took a deep, steady breath in through her nose and let it out through her mouth in an effort to get her heart rate under control. She stretched her right leg, and the pain in her hip faded from a sharp twinge to a dull throb. There was no sound of pursuit, but she dared not peek around the corner and risk giving away her new position. Instead, she stepped off the porch and crossed the street, moving kitty-corner to the next house and on to the back yard.

She moved through the back yards for cover. The desert had long ago reclaimed the ground, returning lawns to dust and desert flora. The remains of a wind chime clinked softly in the breeze, and though she'd likely be the first human being to have heard it in decades, she half expected children to erupt from a nearby door at any moment, or their fathers to come out to investigate the strange woman creeping through their yards.

Most of the homes were identical: small, blocky bungalows cut from the same mold and slapped together in a hurry, no doubt to support the burgeoning silver mine before it went bust. The desert scoured some of them of color, but even in the remainder Angie saw little variety. This one had a concrete stoop, that one a deck, a carport over there. Enough to give a home a hint of personality, but in the end they were all the same prefab crap dropped in a dead and crumbling pop-up town.

Angie chose the home with the collapsed picket fence, thinking maybe, just maybe, it would be enough of an obstacle that her assailants would assume she skipped it. She stepped over the downed rail, and winced as the planks and old nails creaked beneath her weight. Up two steps and across a porch just large enough for a chair and a cigar got her to the back door. The handle twisted back and forth with ease, but the mechanism didn't seem to engage. She turned the handle all the way to the right, braced her shoulder against the door, and pushed.

The wood barked softly as the door popped free of the jamb, then scraped across the tiled floor on the other side. She looked back and forth down the yards one more time, then slipped inside and, with gentle pressure, shoved the door back into the jamb. It didn't close all the way, but made a snug enough fit that someone passing from afar would see no sign of her entry.

Angie allowed herself to relax and limped deeper into the house. There was an old kitchen on her left, stripped of its appliances. A bedroom, a bathroom, and a living room. Her every step kicked up a small cloud of dust, and old webs hung from the corners. It smelled dry and stale, and she swallowed against a tickle in her throat.

Thin, moth-eaten curtains still hung from the front window, one side still secured by its tieback. She stayed a few paces back from it, but close enough she could see the street. She shifted her pistol to her left hand and massaged the front of her hip with her right.

Now that she had at least a few minutes of safety, she reached into her jacket pocket for her cell phone.

The cell phone still connected to the Malibu's cigarette lighter to keep it charged while she used the GPS.

She bit back a curse and kicked up a cloud of dust.

She checked her watch. The sun would set in another hour or so.

Stranded in a ghost town. Hunted by snipers. No way out. Her physical therapist—and the Bureau, for that matter—expected her to be kicking back on a San Diego beach for the next five days.

Fuuuck, me, she thought. It's going to be a long night.

TWO

"DAMN IT, WOMAN, will you get your big ass outta the way of the TV?" Tommy said.

Crystal turned and glared at him. "It's a frickin' commercial, asswipe."

"So what? Maybe I wanna buy a new truck!"

"That'll be the day." She reached above the television and pulled a mixing bowl out of the cabinet. Two smaller bowls tumbled out of it and bounced across the floor. "Those trucks probably cost more than this whole trailer. And I wouldn't have to walk in front of the TV if all these damn boxes weren't in the way!"

"Hey, this is important stuff! The cops would have just taken it all out of Mitch's place and burned it! What else am I supposed to do with it?"

"Oh, I don't know, how about hand the pamphlets out? They don't do any good sitting in boxes, lazy-ass!"

"Shut up, the show's coming back on."

She mumbled something more as she went back into the kitchen, but he drowned her out with the remote.

Cranking up the volume would have to do until someone invented a way to mute her harpy ass.

Tommy was no dummy. He knew the money wasn't coming in, but he didn't have Mitch's connections. He was always content to be a soldier. Make a few drops, kick a few teeth in, get paid, worry about the rest later. It wasn't his fault Mitch got himself killed.

Tommy grabbed his bowl and his lighter off the lamp table and sparked up. He breathed in deep and let it out slow.

"You best save some of that for me!" Crystal snapped.

"Shut the fuck up, I'm thinkin'."

"Yeah, well, don't strain nothin'."

Tommy believed in the Aryan cause. He really did. It was a lot easier to follow than lead, though. Slinging a little meth made ends meet, but it wasn't a fraction of the cash they brought in a few months ago. Mitch and Duff, they made shit happen. They had ideas. Plans. Goals.

Maybe he should have paid a little more attention, shown a little more ambition.

He took another long hit off the bowl. The other guys, they expected more out of him. He could see them drifting away, losing faith. The whispers, the sidelong glances, the sarcastic remarks . . . it all pointed to the end.

Crystal was no different. Used to be they'd party most every night. Now she was always working, always tired, always bitching about how he was smoking her weed. Just because she picked it up and brought it home, suddenly she can't share.

Fuck it. One more hit for inspiration. He held the smoke as he set the bowl and lighter aside again.

He needed to earn again. Bring in that cash, he'd have her respect again. Get out of this trailer and into a proper place. Bury her in bling. Or maybe just bury her. Either way, he'd be back to partying in no time. He leaned over and snatched a pamphlet out of the box, let his bleary eyes wander over the swastika on the cover.

Maybe Crystal had something there. A rally, that's what they needed. Spread the word, recruit some troops. Build up his own little army, just like Mitch put together. Find his own soldiers and expand his territory.

Yeah.

Oil sizzled in the pan in the kitchen. The aromas of chicken and spices filled the trailer. Tommy's stomach rumbled.

First he had to eat. Yeah. Tomorrow he could get started on the planning. Hopefully she'll make mac 'n' cheese and mashed potatoes with the chicken. Oh, and gravy! Mmm, biscuits, too. His mouth watered.

Tump! Tump! Tump!

"Answer the door, would ya'?"

Crystal threw a spatula on the counter and went to the door. Yeah, he wasn't but eight feet from it himself, but the actress on this dancing show looked mighty fine in that tight, red dress. God bless high definition.

No shadow fell on the narrow, pebbled window mounted in the door. Crystal tried to peek out the window, but they had too much shit stacked in front of it, and condensation on the interior clouded her vision. She wiped some of it away with her fingers, but it didn't help much, just offering a smeared view of the yard. Someone stood at the bottom of the front steps, but she couldn't tell who. He climbed up again as she watched and reached for the door.

Tump! Tump! Tump!

"Quit fuckin' around and open the door already!" Tommy said.

"You expecting anyone?"

He shrugged. "Neighbor's pipes probably froze again. Tell him he shoulda kept his faucet on a trickle. I ain't goin' anywhere."

That couldn't be it, Crystal thought. It wasn't that cold anymore. She released the latch. The exterior door and the interior screen door shared a common hinge and swung outward together. She opened them halfway and leaned to see around the edge.

The visitor ripped the door out of her hand. She grasped the doorframe as she stumbled out, then the visitor punched her in the chest, dead center below her sternum. The blow knocked the wind out of her but stopped her fall, and she stumbled back into the trailer, unable to draw another breath. Searing pain erupted from behind her breastbone. She dropped to her knees.

The visitor stepped into the room and slammed the door shut behind him.

"Hey, man! You can't . . ." Tommy let the words die as he got a good look at the visitor, at his black hoodie and the black bandana over his mouth and nose.

At the bloody knife in his hand.

Tommy had a gun. He knew he did. Where the fuck was it? He pawed at the lamp table, knocking his pipe and lighter and a half-empty can of Bud on the floor.

Crystal gulped for air, finally drawing a few shuddering breaths. Her hand, pressed to her stomach, felt warm and sticky. She looked down, saw the blood covering her palm and covering the belly of her khaki t-shirt. She let out a weak croak of a scream, drew in another ragged breath.

Tommy flipped the table. The bulb in the lamp exploded, casting the end of the living room in shadow and white flickering light from the television. Where the fuck was that gun?

Crystal got out a full scream at last. The visitor grabbed her hair and yanked her head back. His blade sliced across her throat before she could get her hands up. Her scream cut to a gurgle. She clutched at her neck with both hands, tucking her chin in a vain attempt to contain the blood.

Behind the chair! Tommy remembered. He spun the chair to the left and reached back. His hand struck the shotgun's barrel propped against the window behind him. It rolled around the lip of the frame, scraped across the wall, and hit the floor with a clatter. Tommy spun the other direction and watched as the visitor stomp-kicked the center of Crystal's back. Her head snapped back as she fell forward, revealing the gaping wound across her neck. The visitor stepped over her legs and into the living room.

Tommy knew he couldn't beat the guy to the shotgun. He pushed out of his chair and circled toward the television. His hand found the folding knife in his front pocket. He pulled it out, shoved the small knob at the base of the blade with his thumb. The spring assist took over, and the blade flashed open with a solid click.

The visitor's narrowed eyes betrayed the smile behind the bandana over his face. He settled into a fighting stance, the knife low in his right hand, his left up in a guard position.

Tommy licked his lips. His knife was longer than the visitor's. Heavier. He could do this. He took a tentative step forward. The visitor didn't react. He jabbed a low feint, then raised his knife high for a downward slash.

The visitor stepped inside his reach and put up his left arm to catch Tommy's wrist on his forearm. A quick twist and he had Tommy's wrist locked up in an iron grip. His knife flicked once across the inside of Tommy's forearm, then twice across his body.

Tommy hissed with each cut and jumped back. His heel struck a box, and he almost went over backward. He couldn't feel his knife in his grip any more, and a squashed X across his chest oozed blood.

"Try again." The visitor pointed to the floor.

Tommy looked down at his own knife lying near his foot. He could barely close the fingers of his right hand. He crouched down and picked up the knife with his left hand, keeping his eye on the visitor the whole time. He rose and matched the visitor's stance.

"Who the fuck are you?" Tommy asked.

"The man putting you out of business."

"Do you know who I am? Who my friends are? They'll never stop looking for you!"

"I'm shakin'."

Tommy lunged forward, leading with the knife. The visitor twisted to one side and made a quick downward slash across Tommy's left wrist. Tommy yelped, then grunted as the visitor's left elbow caught him on the bridge of the nose. Tears filled his eyes and stars exploded across his vision. The visitor spun him around. One, two, three jabs to his kidney lit up his back with pain. One more stab between the ribs for good measure, and the visitor shoved him away.

He collapsed to his knees and propped himself up on his chair. He couldn't draw the breath to scream. It felt like someone parked a car on his chest. His side and back burned. Hot blood cascaded down the back of his leg. Black closed in around the edges of his vision as he craned his neck to see the intruder crouching down beside him.

"This is Sword territory now," the man said.

Tommy blinked. He couldn't muster the strength to move. The knife slipped from his fingers, hit the floor with a soft thump. The pain faded and grew distant.

His last breath hitched in his throat.

THREE

THE OLD DIESEL PICKUP RUMBLED through the desert at better than seventy miles an hour. Its high-beams slashed the darkness, yet barely picked out the old road surface beneath the sand and dirt. It didn't seem to bother Sheriff Jerome Hess as he steered the truck through the occasional curves with ease. He marked off the miles with measured puffs of the cigar clenched between his teeth. The smoke filled the cabin and threatened to choke out his passenger, Cole Tyler, riding shotgun.

The cigar stank of stale earth and faded leather, a scent Cole would forever associate with the old bastard next to him. Middle age had softened the sheriff's muscles, but he more than made up for it with a hardened tempter. His stout paunch and soft features gave him a jolly, affable look, but anyone he pulled over would soon find that wasn't the case. The two years since Cole last saw the man did little to take the edge off, and added a few more wrinkles to his weathered hide. The pepper had shaken loose from his hair, leaving only dingy gray and dirty white.

Jesus, Cole thought. Two years already? He wondered how different things would be—if he would be sitting here right now—had he blown the sheriff's brains out that night. Marcus Rice may have been responsible for the death of Cole's brother, Will, but Hess had pulled the trigger. Letting Hess live was the smart play, but deep down Cole often questioned whether it was the right play.

Cole opened his window six inches, letting the dense smoke out and the cool air in. The landscape looked as barren and dead as the snow-covered wilderness back home. At least the landscape back home would be coming back to life in the next few weeks.

He stifled a yawn. A sleepless night and an early flight left him drained. If he hadn't taken the time to down a few sandwiches before Hess picked him up at the motel, he'd really be in bad shape.

"It wasn't a call for help, you know." Hess rolled down his window and tossed out the stub of his cigar. "My men and I can handle this."

"I know," Cole said. "This isn't about trust. It's personal."

"Fair enough. I just called because . . . well, because I owe you. That's all."

Damn right he did. Cole suspected that was as close as Hess would come to offering an apology.

"Marcus Rice was a lot of things, but to kill his own brother and frame yours? Ain't nobody saw that comin'. Charlie Rice was a damn good man, not a thing like Marcus."

Shit. The only thing worse than a half-assed apology? An explanation. Cole rubbed his nose to hide his scowl.

"When I found Charlie all tore up in his own home like that . . . I guess it tore me up some, too. I let it get personal, and Marcus's explanation was the easy one."

And there it was. But it didn't explain why Kate had to die, too. Why Cole and his mother had to cook up a bullshit story for her father, and accept responsibility for her death because she eloped with Will.

"I have to wonder, Sheriff, how many other innocents you've got buried out in this desert."

"Because of Marcus?"

"Because you were all tore up over something."

Hess chuckled. "Fair enough. Let's just say you're the first to come looking for any of 'em."

Silence fell between them for the next mile.

"Listen," Hess said then, "I've been meaning to ask you somethin'. Ever since Marcus bit me, I've been having some nasty dreams. If you bite someone, does it, you know, change them?"

"No."

"You sure? I mean, how did you become . . . the way you are?"

"I was born this way," Cole said. "Same as my brother, and same, I imagine, as the Rice brothers."

"Huh."

"Do you have any idea whether Charlie Rice had any native blood in him?"

"Yeah. A couple generations back, I think. I take it you're full blood?"

"Yeah."

"Never did take you for an Irishman."

Cole laughed.

"Why, does Indian blood have something to do with it?" Hess asked.

"I have no idea." It wasn't a lie. Mom didn't have a lot of answers, and he never got the chance to ask his father.

"Huh," Hess said again. "As it happens, Charlie Rice was full of surprises. But we're here. We can talk more about that later."

Wonderful, Cole thought.

Hess tapped the brakes. They rode past the crumbled remains of a wooden sign and the headlights fell on the sides of a pair of brick buildings flanking the road. The street and buildings alike were dark. Hess turned off the high beams.

"We're here."

"Where's 'here'?"

"Charity. It's another old mining town."

"Where is everyone?"

"About fifty years back, the mining company went chasing a bad seam. The explosion triggered a sinkhole on the north side of town, which swallowed half a block and killed a couple dozen people. Two days later, three more people died and they figured out they screwed up the well, too. Between the unsteady ground and the poisoned water, the people couldn't leave fast enough."

"So you had Wallace sent out here for a nice, private chat?"

A man in desert camouflage walked out into the path of the headlights. He held a shotgun in his right hand, the butt resting under his ribs and the barrel pointed skyward. He waved down the pickup with his other hand.

"We're about to find out." Hess stopped the pickup a few feet short of the man and killed the engine. He left the headlights on as he climbed out.

Cole got out on the other side. He sized up the man with the shotgun. The guy was tall, maybe six inches taller than the sheriff. Dark red hair peeked out from beneath his khaki baseball cap, and a red beard filled out his jaw. His arms and face were lean, and Cole realized the padding he'd first taken as muscle was a bulletproof vest.

There were two neat holes in the man's shirt, right over his left pectoral muscle.

"What have we got, Harv?" Hess asked him.

"There's a problem, Boss. We've lost her somewhere in town."

"Goddamn it. This was supposed to be a simple job!"

"I know, but she was armed!"

"Of course she was armed," Cole said. "She's a federal agent."

Hess and his man exchanged a glance.

"And why the fuck didn't you tell me this on the phone last night?"

"You mean she didn't identify herself that way?" Cole asked.

"Hell no. We'd be handling this a lot differently if we knew she was a goddamn fed!"

Strange, Cole thought. She should have announced herself to the sheriff when she first arrived. What was she up to?

"Where is she now?"

"We're not sure," Harvey said. "But she's not going anywhere! Check it out." He reached into the large cargo pocket on the side of his thigh and pulled out a chunky cell phone and a key ring with a key, a black plastic fob, and a white rental tag on it.

Cole looked over at the car sitting at the end of the block, not quite past the reach of Hess's headlights. He noticed both tires on the passenger side had blown out, and the front end had ground onto the sidewalk.

Hess took the phone and keys and stuffed them in the pocket of his vest. "You still haven't answered my question."

"We didn't expect her to shoot back. I tried to put a scare into her with the shotgun, and she put me on my ass." He touched a finger to one of the bullet holes in his shirt. "Then she ran off down a side street and we lost her."

"What have you been doing since? Where the hell is Sam?"

"We looked for her, but when it started getting dark we stashed the Jeep and took watch on her car. Sam's up on the roof."

"How far's the nearest town?" Cole asked.

"Sunset's twenty-two miles back," Hess said. "That's it."

"Then she isn't going anywhere."

"How do you know that?"

"Because she's got a bad hip."

"Yeah, she left a cane in the car, too," Harvey said.

Hess spat a thick glob of phlegm on the street. "Just how well do you know this woman, Tyler?"

Cole shrugged. "There was an incident back home last fall, and she took a bullet. I haven't talked to her since, but I doubt she's in any shape to run a marathon."

"Well, we have no choice now." Hess drew his pistol from his hip holster and checked the chamber, then returned it to his hip. "We need to find her and finish the job."

"Not before I talk to her," Cole said. "You know I can find her, but I need to know what she's doing here and what she knows."

He felt some relief the Bureau may not have sent her. That didn't mean they wouldn't come looking for her if she disappeared, though. And if the Bureau didn't send her down on a lead, then what was her angle?

Hess took off his cowboy hat and smoothed his hair. He fiddled with the brim of the hat for a moment. "It's gonna be a lot harder to take her alive, assuming we even find her."

"She's in the middle of the desert with no food or water. She's got to come out sometime."

"Alright, here's how we'll play it. I'm going to call in a few more guys. We'll spread out, flush her out. We catch her, you get first crack at her. But if she doesn't come quietly and catches a bullet . . ." Hess shrugged. "Shit happens."

"All I ask is we try."

"Then I guess I've got some calls to make." Hess put his hat back on and returned to the truck.

Cole extended a hand to the man with the shotgun. "Cole Tyler."

"Jim Harvey." He took Cole's hand in a firm grip, pumped it once.

"Are you a deputy?"

"Yep. You're the guy who took down Marcus Rice?"

"That's right."

Harvey nodded. "Son of a bitch had it coming. Charlie was good people. Any man who kills his own kin deserves to be put down."

He grunted a vague affirmative. "I'm going to go check out the car."

Harvey made a go-ahead gesture toward the car.

Cole took a short leather cord out of his pocket and tied his hair back into a tail to keep it out of his face while he worked. The end hung down between his shoulder blades.

He approached the car from the sidewalk to keep his shadow off if. Hess's guys sure did a job on her: flat tires, shattered windows, bullet holes in the quarter panel and hood. He opened the driver's side door and the dome light came on. No blood on the seat, or anywhere else on the interior that he could see. He slipped inside.

A barrage of scents struck him: the fake new car smell the detailers used between rentals; the stale cigarette smoke lingering in the ceiling fabric; the rotten bits of food the vacuum missed between the seat and the console; the hint of cocoa butter-infused hotel shampoo in the head rest. That last had to be Agent Wallace, or the cleansers would have overwhelmed it.

Now he had her scent. If only he could read her intent as easily . . .

FROM

LIE WITH THE DEAD

By Mike Oliveri

ABOUT THE AUTHOR

Mike Oliveri was raised in the Chicago suburbs, but currently resides near Peoria, Illinois, where it's impossible to get a good Italian beef sandwich. In his free time, he studies Shuri-ryu Karate. As of this writing, he is a first-degree black belt.

Mike's novel, *Deadliest of the Species*, won the Horror Writers Association's Bram Stoker Award for Superior Achievement in a First Novel for works published in 2001. Since then, Mike has published a handful of novellas and several short stories, participated in a web serial, and dabbled in tech-oriented non-fiction. He vows his next novel will not be a trunk novel.

You can learn more about Mike and his work at his website, mikeoliveri.com.

ABOUT EVILEYE BOOKS

Evileye Books publishes horror, dark fiction, crime, supernatural thrillers, and science fiction. For more information please visit our website, Evileyebooks.com.

If you share our love of stories that consume you, consider some of our titles out now:

Bone Welder
By Ray Bradbury Award winner Greg Kishbaugh

DarkWalker
by John Urbancik

Creeping Stones
By New York Times best-selling author Cullen Bunn

Never Bet the Devil & Other Warnings
By Orrin Grey

The Dead Sheriff: Zombie Damnation
By Mark Justice

The Burning Maiden Anthology
Edited by Greg Kishbaugh

Featuring award winning
best-selling authors

Joe R. Lansdale

Matthew Pearl

Charles Johnson

Lyndsay Faye

Louis Bayard

Mort Castle

Sarah Langan

Bruce Boston

Cullen Bunn

Steven Barnes

www.ingramcontent.com/pod-product-compliance
Lightning Source LLC
Chambersburg PA
CBHW030134180626
46812CB00002B/686